DO NOT MESS WITH THE MERMAIDS

Books by Michelle Robinson

Do Not Disturb the Dragons
Do Not Mess with the Mermaids

Michelle Robinson

DO NOT MESS WITH THE MERMAIDS

Illustrated by
Sharon Davey

BLOOMSBURY
CHILDREN'S BOOKS
LONDON OXFORD NEW YORK NEW DELHI SYDNEY

BLOOMSBURY CHILDREN'S BOOKS
Bloomsbury Publishing Plc
50 Bedford Square, London WC1B 3DP, UK
29 Earlsfort Terrace, Dublin 2, Ireland

BLOOMSBURY, BLOOMSBURY CHILDREN'S BOOKS
and the Diana logo are trademarks of Bloomsbury Publishing Plc

First published in Great Britain in 2021 by Bloomsbury Publishing Plc

A catalogue record for this book is available from the British Library

ISBN: PB: 978-1-4088-9491-0; eBook: 978-1-4088-9490-3

Printed by ... .td,

To find out ... bury.com

To the Platt family – see you over the moat!
– MR

To Neve and Alex, always
– SD

CONTENTS

1

DO NOT SWIM IN PURPLE WATER

The sign was almost as big as the castle drawbridge.

It was hard to miss. Although you *might not* spot it if you'd never visited Wondermere Castle before.

In that case you'd be so busy admiring the dragons in their turret-top nests, you wouldn't notice the state of the castle moat.

Not only was it surrounded by warning signs, but the water in it had turned the most shocking shade of purple.

It bothered the moat's resident mermaids. They'd packed their things and gone to stay in nearby Lake Wonder. It bothered the king. He was expecting very important visitors and wanted the castle to look its best. But it didn't bother his daughter. Then again, nothing really bothered Princess Grace.

She'd arrived on the orphan cart at just two years old, taken one look at the dragons' nests and climbed up the nearest turret to get a better look. She'd broken several of Wondermere's rigid rules in the space of just five minutes, getting covered in sparkling dragon poo while she was at it. But at least she hadn't disturbed the dragons. Everyone agreed she must have the most astonishingly good luck.

And perhaps Grace really *was* lucky, because, as the next eight years passed, she got away with breaking just about every rule in Wondermere's very old-fashioned book – and there were certainly plenty of rules to break.

Princesses do not wear armour. Princesses do not ride unicorns. Princesses do not sneakily enter the annual Troll-o Tournament – and they *definitely* do not win it.

Grace had been there, done that and got the trophy, accompanied by her smart and caring sister, Princess Portia. King Wonder had to admit that his daughters' rule breaking hadn't done the dragons any harm. In fact, they seemed happier than ever. They'd even started laying eggs, and their nests were overflowing with plump baby dragons.

If the dragons were happy, the princesses were happier still. They'd been knighted by the king – the first girls ever to become *sirs* – and each was now in charge of something truly important.

As Champion of Dragon Studies, Sir Portia's job was to keep an eye on dragon behaviour, and, as Champion of Troll-o, Sir Grace helped other girls train and play with the boys for the first time in history.

Troll-o was the nation's favourite sport, and Grace lived for it. She loved nothing better than to put on her armour, mount her unicorn and chase after the ball-troll, mallet in hand. As captain of the league, she was in her element. No wonder people called her the luckiest girl in the kingdom. But was she lucky enough to get away with swimming in forbidden purple water … ?

'I only want a little dip,' Grace said as she rode Poop, her disobedient unicorn, through the castle courtyard towards the main gates. 'A swim in the moat after troll-o practice is practically tradition.'

'I thought you hated tradition?' said Portia with a smile. She was riding beside Grace on her beautifully turned out unicorn, Sprinkles. As ever, she was riding hands-free and reading a book about dragons.

Worn out from practice, Poop's hooves plodded heavily across the cobbles. But Grace knew better than to ask him to speed up. Her grumpy, grotty steed always did the exact opposite of what he was told. Thankfully she knew exactly how to handle him. 'Take your time, boy, I'm in no hurry for a swim.'

Poop pricked up his ears, gave a mischievous snort and shot out of the castle gates, dumping Grace into the moat with a **SPLOOSH!**

Portia urged Sprinkles into a trot and caught up, coming to a stop on the drawbridge. 'Dad'll go mad if he catches you,' she called down to Grace. 'Our guests will be arriving any minute! No one from the Outer Ocean has ever visited Wondermere before. You know how important it is we make a good impression.'

Grace spat out a mouthful of purple water. 'They're merfolk,' she said, 'and not just any merfolk. They're champion swimmers! I bet they'll be glad to see we like water too – isn't that right, Poop?' Poop gave a bored snort and began to nibble on a patch of pixie wort.

Portia looked longingly at the water. 'Dad *did* say this visit's all about showing our guests how much we value their customs ...'

'You should join me,' Grace suggested, treading water as she tugged off her armour. 'Although I'd recommend getting changed *before* jumping in. If my troll-o kit goes rusty, I'm blaming Poop!'

Portia bit her lip. 'What's the water like? Does it feel any different to normal?'

Grace peered into the moat's purple depths. 'It feels great,' she said.

It really did feel good. Grace was hot and sticky from the morning's troll-o practice. She and Poop had scored three goals, much to the delight of the ball-troll, who loved nothing better than being whacked on the bottom by a mallet. Grace loved whacking them, too – although it did make her arms ache. A quick swim would soon fix that.

She floated lazily along on her back and gazed up at the castle turrets. The adult dragons were teaching their new babies how to fly.

Up on the bank, Portia tucked her reading book into her saddlebag, took out some parchment and a quill and began taking notes. She soon forgot all about the visitors, allowing herself to become completely absorbed by the dragons. 'They're absolutely fascinating,' she said, resting her quill to watch.

An enormous blue dragon nudged its baby gently to the edge of its nest, then gave it a good, hard shove.

The girls gasped. For a heart-stopping

instant it looked as though
the little dragon would
plummet to the ground.
But at the last moment it
flapped its wings and soared
skyward, turning joyful cartwheels
above the moat.

SPLAT! The little dragon's glittery
dung hit Grace right in the eye.

'UGH!' she cried, flailing about
in the water. 'Why does that
always happen to me?!'

Portia laughed. 'Don't complain,
you know it's supposed to be
lucky!'

'It's also *gross*,' Grace
grumbled, splashing
about to wash off the mess.

'Tell me more about the water,' Portia said, licking the tip of her quill. 'Does it still taste like sugar lumps?'

Grace was busy rinsing dragon dung out of her hair. 'Right now it tastes kind of poopy.'

'How about the temperature?' Portia asked. 'Is it hotter? Colder?'

Grace frowned. 'Now you mention it, it *does* feel kind of warm ...'

The water around Grace began to bubble. 'You're disgusting,' said Portia.

'It wasn't *me*,' Grace said, her eyes widening. 'I think there's something else in here ...'

'Get out, quick!' Portia held out a hand.

'No chance,' Grace said. 'I want to find out what it is!' She took a deep breath, kicked hard and swam down into the moat's murky, purple depths.

2

DO NOT TOUCH
A DRAGON'S EGG

Grace kept her eyes open as she dived deeper, following the steady stream of bubbles.

Maybe they had something to do with the water's unusual colour? There was only one way to find out.

The moat felt oddly empty with its mermaids gone, but its sandy bottom was still strewn with coins and jewels that had been accidentally dropped by the dragons or kicked out of their nests over the centuries.

As Grace swam, shy water nymphs darted out of her way, hiding among strings of brilliant blue bogweed. On any other day she might have tried to catch them, but there was no time for that. She'd noticed a large spotted egg lying cushioned in the soft sand.

There was no mistaking it – it was a dragon's egg. She'd seen them close up once before. Although dragons' eggs didn't normally *glow* ... Perhaps this one was broken? There was the tiniest crack in its side, and out of the crack came bubble after bubble.

Touching a dragon's egg was forbidden, but

Grace couldn't resist. It was glowing so
brightly she had to squint as she reached out
and carefully picked it up. She gasped,
letting out a stream of bubbles of her own.
The egg had a heartbeat. Portia *had* to see
this! Grace clutched the egg to her chest and
kicked hard for the surface.

The egg was large and heavy. Portia helped Grace roll it out of the moat and on to the grassy bank.

'Careful,' Portia said, her eyes wide and twinkling with pleasure. 'No one's touched a dragon's egg before, you might damage it.' She dried her hands on her dress, picked up her quill and began making a sketch of the egg.

Grace clambered on to the bank and started pulling her armour back on over her wet Under-Wonders. 'I haven't damaged it, it has a heartbeat,' she said, tugging on her breastplate. 'Anyway, it was already broken when I found it. See? There's a little crack in it; it's where all those bubbles were coming from. I swear it was glowing before. Perhaps

I was imagining things?'

'Maybe I'm imagining things too,' Portia said, 'but isn't the water looking a little less purple?'

Grace frowned. 'Maybe, just a bit.'

Portia pushed her glasses up her nose and pointed to the nearest turret. 'It must have rolled out of that nest. Its poor parents must be worried sick! We ought to leave it here on the bank. Maybe they'll find it and pick it up?'

Grace didn't reply. She'd just begun to drift into a lovely daydream about keeping a pet dragon when a voice squeaked out behind her, making her jump.

'Ah, princesses! Getting ready to welcome our visitors, are we?'

It was Taffy Trafalgar, the king's

right-hand troll and the girls' tutor. He came
bustling out of the castle gates, accompanied
by Sir Oliver and Sir Arthur. Grace quickly
tugged Portia's cloak from her shoulders and
tossed it over the egg.

'What in all Wonder …?' began Sir Arthur,
but he hadn't noticed the egg. He was simply
watching Grace drip. 'Did you fall in the
purple water?!'

Sir Oliver gave Grace a concerned look.
'Are you feeling all right, princess?'

'Oh, I haven't been in the moat,' Grace
fibbed. 'I just had a shower after troll-o.'

Sir Arthur looked puzzled. 'In your *clothes*?'

'They needed a wash, too.'

Taffy Trafalgar was hopping excitedly
from one long, rabbity foot to the other.
'Excellent thinking, your highness. We all

need to be well turned out today. We mustn't give our visitors a bad impression. Boys, take down all the warning signs!'

The boys bowed to the princesses and got to work.

'You may as well leave the signs up,' Grace said, wringing out her hair. 'The visitors are hardly going to miss the fact the water's bright purple.'

'With any luck they'll be so busy admiring the dragons they won't notice,' Taffy said, foot thumping the ground impatiently. 'Besides, the knights will line up to greet them and keep the worst of it hidden. Now go and put on your frilliest dresses! Queen Jeen and her waterfolly squad are expected any minute and we need you at your best.'

Grace sighed. 'I'm at my best in armour, not skirts.'

'Please, princess,' Taffy said, tugging at his ears. 'The merfolk have never been further inland than the Western Beaches. This is the first time they've ever set fin on soil. It's an epic moment in Wondermerian history!'

'The goal I scored earlier was pretty epic

too,' Grace said grumpily, 'and I did it in a perfectly good suit of armour.'

'You absolutely walloped that troll,' Sir Arthur said. Taffy glared at him, so he got back to work helping Sir Oliver take down an enormous **OUT OF BOUNDS** sign.

Taffy wagged a hairy finger at Grace. 'Complain all you want, but remember: it's *your* efforts to promote troll-o that brought our visitors here in the first place.'

Grace rolled her eyes, but in truth she felt proud. She'd turned what was already a popular sport into a real craze. The whole realm was abuzz with troll-o fever! No wonder the merfolk wanted to see what all the fuss was about.

Taffy took Grace's hand in his paws and looked her in the eye. 'The merfolk are coming to learn about our legendary pluck and team spirit. As Champion of Troll-o, your father expects you to show that more than anyone.'

Grace sighed. 'I know.'

'You can wear armour for the exhibition match later tonight, but please,' he begged, '*please* go and put on a dress?'

'Fine,' Grace said, rolling her eyes. 'But not a frilly one.'

'Don't worry, Taffy,' Portia said, giving the old troll her sweetest smile. 'We'll be beautifully turned out in no time.'

'And no mischief?' Taffy added anxiously.

'No mischief,' Grace said, carefully scooping up Portia's cloak and the egg that was hidden inside it.

3

NEVER SNEEZE ON ROYALTY

The girls took their unicorns to the royal stables, then trudged up the winding stone staircase to their room.

Grace kept the dragon's egg hidden. If Portia saw it, she'd want to return it to the moat-side for its parents to find. But what if they didn't? What if the egg was left alone and unguarded, with no one in the whole realm to take care of it?

Grace didn't want to risk it. From the moment she'd felt its heart beating in her hands, she'd known she would do anything to keep it safe. She tucked it carefully beneath her bedcovers, then quickly swapped her armour for her least frilly dress. There was no time to dry or brush her hair. She linked arms with Portia and went to join their father in the Great Hall.

'There you are, girls,' said the king. 'I was beginning to think you'd sneaked off into the forest on one of your jaunts.' King Wonder gave Grace a puzzled look. 'Why is your hair dripping wet?'

'Um ...' Grace bit her lip as she searched for an explanation.

'Because she wanted to make our visitors

feel at home,' Portia said. Grace gave her sister a grateful look.

'Goodness,' said their father, looking taken aback, 'how surprisingly thoughtful of you.'

Taffy Trafalgar came bouncing up to the royal thrones. 'They're here!' he squeaked excitedly. 'The visitors are here!'

'And the moat … ?' said King Wonder anxiously.

Taffy's chest swelled with pride. 'The knights closed ranks, held up their shields and kept it entirely hidden from the merfolk's view. We got away with it, your highness!'

The king smiled broadly. 'Excellent work,' he said, straightening his crown as a loud fanfare echoed around the Great Hall. Grace watched, astonished, as Sir Oliver and Sir Arthur marched in waving flags. They were followed closely by Queen Jeen, ruler of the Outer Ocean, and the waterfolly squad she famously captained. Grace counted five mermen and thirteen mermaids in total, each gliding smoothly over the flagstone floor in their own wheeled chariot.

The only chariots Grace had ever seen were great big things pulled by unicorns. These ones weren't much bigger than bathtubs, but they were much, *much* fancier.

Each chariot was shaped like a giant seashell, and each one glistened as though it had just been pulled from the sea. The merqueen headed the procession in the fanciest chariot of all. She sat waist-deep in water inside a beautiful coiled conch, the same soft pink colour as ripe bogberries. Grace couldn't help but admire it.

'Wondermere welcomes our honoured guests,' Sir Oliver announced loudly, giving his flag a swish and accidentally wrapping it around Sir Arthur's face.

'Mmphh-nng-rrfff-huur-mrrmph—!' announced Sir Arthur, finally untangling himself. 'All hail Queen Jeen!'

Queen Jeen rode straight up to the king, offering him her delicate, scaled hand. Grace shook hands, too, trying not to gawp at the merqueen's blue hair, which streamed over her shoulders like a waterfall. 'Greetings from the Outer Ocean,' Queen Jeen said prettily.

'Wonderful to meet you, your highness,' said King Wonder with a bow. 'We hope your stay here will be a—'

'A ... aaa ... AA-TISHOO!'

Grace's sneeze sprayed all over the merqueen and echoed round the Great Hall.

Taffy gasped and hid behind his long ears. **'Never sneeze on royalty!'**

'Sorry,' Grace said, wiping her nose on her sleeve. 'Wet hair.'

King Wonder offered Queen Jeen a handkerchief. 'My daughters are keen to make sure you feel at home during your stay,'

he said, giving Grace a disapproving look.
'May I introduce them properly? This is Sir
Portia, Champion of Dragon Studies, and Sir
Grace, Champion of Troll-o.'

Queen Jeen raised an eyebrow. 'Ah, yes,
your famous *troll-o*,' she said snootily. 'Your
new mixed league is all they're talking about
at the coast. Of course our own beloved
waterfolly has *always* been played by both

boys and girls, so I don't really see what all the fuss is about.'

'We look forward to watching you play during your visit,' said the king, 'just as I'm sure *you* are looking forward to this evening's troll-o exhibition match. You'll soon see why it's so popular. It really is the most thrilling sport.'

Queen Jeen raised a single blue eyebrow. 'I'll believe it when I see it.'

Grace scoffed. 'I suppose you think waterfolly's better?'

'Manners!' the king hissed. But Queen Jeen waved a hand dismissively.

'Absolutely. There's no sport as exhilarating or as elegant. Hitting trolls with a mallet sounds rather loutish to me.'

'Loutish?' Grace said, disgusted. 'Troll-o's nothing of the sort!'

The merqueen wrinkled her nose. 'I'll be the judge of that. Right now my squad needs to settle in and practise. We're not used to playing in fresh water. It'll take some getting used to.'

'Of course,' said King Wonder, 'but perhaps you'd like the castle tour first?'

'We can start with the flying buttresses,' Taffy said excitedly. 'The oldest one is eight hundred and sixty-three years old!'

'The tour can wait,' said Queen Jeen. 'We

train for seven hours every day, without fail. I hear your knights only train for three? Dedication is key.'

Grace's cheeks flushed pink. 'My knights are extremely dedicated!'

''Tis true,' said Sir Oliver loyally, 'we got up at nine o'clock this morning just to polish our mallets.'

'Nine o'clock?' scoffed Queen Jeen. 'We rise at six.'

Grace was turning from pink to a furious shade of red. Portia spoke up before her sister could say anything she might regret. 'Goodness, that's marvellous. We're both looking forward to picking up some tips from you and your squad during your stay. Right, Grace?'

Grace gritted her teeth. 'Right.'

Queen Jeen didn't look convinced.

'We are honoured to have you here,' King Wonder said, smiling warmly at his guests, 'and I know we'll be just as delighted by your waterfolly as you will be by our own troll-o. Now, why don't we get you settled in to the royal baths so you can relax and begin to enjoy the wonders that Wondermere has to offer?'

'We don't relax, and we couldn't possibly stay in the royal baths. Swimming indoors? I don't think so, not when you have a perfectly fine moat outside.'

'You can't stay in the moat,' Taffy said, hopping from foot to foot. 'The moat is—'

Queen Jeen stared down her nose at him. 'The moat is where we'll be staying, hairy butler. My squad is keen to see it. We've heard great things about it from our onshore cousins.'

The merfolk began nodding and murmuring their approval.

King Wonder looked appalled. 'But it … it's …'

'The perfect shape for a waterfolly track, precisely,' said the merqueen. 'If your knights would be so kind as to escort us there at once? These twisting corridors all look the same to me.'

Portia gave Grace an anxious look as Sir Oliver and Sir Arthur led the visitors back out of the Great Hall, accompanied by a flustered King Wonder and a panicky Taffy. Portia turned to Grace and whispered, 'When she sees the water's purple she's going to flip!'

Grace grinned. 'Come on,' she said, grabbing her sister's hand. 'That's got to be worth watching.'

4

DO NOT POOP
IN A MERMAID'S MOAT

The royal family had to jog to keep up with the merfolk's chariots.

'You ought to at least *see* the royal baths first,' King Wonder called after them as they sped out through the castle gates. 'We've spent all week preparing them. I'm sure you'd prefer them to the moat, which is pur ... pur ...'

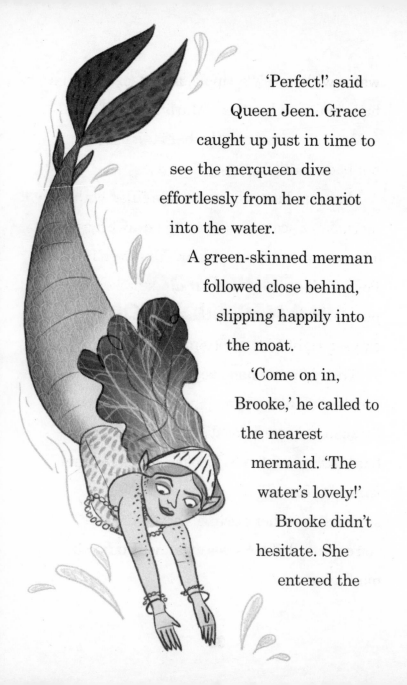

'Perfect!' said
Queen Jeen. Grace
caught up just in time to
see the merqueen dive
effortlessly from her chariot
into the water.

A green-skinned merman
followed close behind,
slipping happily into
the moat.

'Come on in,
Brooke,' he called to
the nearest
mermaid. 'The
water's lovely!'

Brooke didn't
hesitate. She
entered the

water with barely a ripple, resurfacing with a huge smile on her face. 'Marlin's right,' she said to her friends on the bank. 'It's really not bad at all!'

Moments later, the moat was filled with merfolk. Grace peered over the drawbridge. The water was crystal clear. 'You were right, Portia,' she said quietly, 'it *did* stop being purple when I took out the egg. Look! You can see right to the bottom!'

'The egg must have been causing the problem all along,' Portia whispered, gazing down at the merfolk. 'Well, it's not on the bank where we left it. Looks like its parents found it after all.'

Grace gave her sister a wicked grin.

Portia rolled her eyes. 'Oh, no. Don't tell me you kept it?'

Grace ignored her.

'It really is a surprisingly pleasing moat,' said Queen Jeen, smiling charmingly up from the water.

'*Surprising* is exactly the word for it,' said King Wonder, relieved. 'We hope you'll all be very comfortable here.'

'You get the best view of the dragons in the whole realm,' said Portia, pointing up to the turrets. 'Aren't they amazing?'

Brooke and Marlin shared a look. 'If you say so,' said Marlin rudely.

'They *are* amazing,' said Grace matter-of-factly. 'And it's an even better view than normal. Dad had all the honeysuckle and ivy stripped away to make the castle look tidier for you.'

'*Tidier?*' said Brooke, wrinkling her nose

at the scruffy nests on top of the turrets. A large red dragon sat in the nearest one, playing with its baby. The little dragon shrieked happily, then stuck its bottom over the edge of the nest and – **FLUP!** It deposited a glittering stream of poo into the moat.

'You missed me!' Grace laughed, but her smile faded as another dragon flew overhead, scoring a bullseye. **SPLAT!**

'Bravo, princess!' Sir Arthur cheered, looking her up and down admiringly. 'You really do have the most marvellous luck!'

Meanwhile the merfolk were swimming as fast as they could for the bank, heading rapidly back into their chariots. 'How utterly revolting,' said Queen Jeen. 'How on earth can your local mermaids bear to live in such foul water?'

Sir Oliver looked thoroughly puzzled. 'You think dragon dung is *foul*?'

Sir Arthur eyed Grace's filthy dress enviously. 'Why, every last drop is a glorious, luck-drenched treasure!'

'You should try bathing in it, boys,' Grace said cheekily. 'You'll need all the luck you can get if you want *your team* to beat *my team* in the troll-o tonight.'

'Ah, yes! The exhibition match starts in two hours,' said King Wonder, glad of an opportunity to shift the attention away from the dragons. 'How about we leave our honoured guests to freshen up and settle in—?'

'Settle in?!' Queen Jeen barked. 'How on earth are we supposed to settle beneath those filthy, fidgeting flappers?!'

'They're not filthy,' said Portia, 'and their dirt has natural healing powers.'

'Besides,' said Grace, wringing dung from her hair, 'it's only natural.'

Just then a baby dragon flew by, turning loop the loops over the startled visitors' heads. Queen Jeen shrieked, ducking under the surface for cover with the rest of her squad.

Grace sneered. 'Wimps,' she whispered, but a stern look from her father stopped her from saying any more.

'They're so skittish and unpredictable,' said the merqueen, looking horrified as another dragon skimmed the surface of the moat. 'We can't possibly stay here. Perhaps this visit isn't such a good idea after all?'

'Let's not be too hasty,' said King Wonder. 'I know you're not *super* keen on the idea of an indoor pool, but I really do believe you'll be very comfortable in the royal baths.'

'Are there any dragons indoors?' said Queen Jeen suspiciously.

Taffy stood to attention, cleared his throat and said proudly, 'You can search the history books and you'll not find a single instance of dragons entering Wondermere Castle.

Believe me, I've read every last book and scroll.'

'Not a single dragon? Ever?' asked Queen Jeen.

'Not even a little one,' said King Wonder confidently.

Queen Jeen sniffed. 'In that case I suppose we could give it a try. But no official business tonight, please. We're all stressed and need some proper time in water.'

'No troll-o?! You absolute—' Grace said. She was about to call the merqueen a very rude name, but King Wonder interrupted.

'Troll-o can wait. Let's get you all well and truly settled in and comfortable,' he said. 'Sir Arthur, lead the way!'

Portia made to follow after the procession of chariots, but Grace grabbed her arm and held her back. 'Hang on a minute,' she said. 'If that snooty lot are staying in the baths, where are all us knights going to clean up when we finally *do* get to play troll-o?'

Portia shrugged. 'The moat?'

Grace put on a hoity-toity voice. 'But I can't face getting dragon poo in my beautiful hair!'

Portia laughed. 'I think it's a bit late for that. Come on, let's go get you cleaned up – plus I want you to tell me what you've done with that egg.'

Grace grinned. 'Race you!' she said, lifting her skirts and sprinting off towards their room.

5

DO NOT TICKLE
A GRUMPY UNICORN

Grace found it hard to relax with visitors in the castle, so she was glad to get back to her room. The bedchamber she shared with Portia was cosy and private. Best of all, there was no need to act like a princess.

She tugged off her dress, pulled on her favourite tunic and a pair of trousers, and flopped into an armchair in front of the fire.

A serving troll had laid out extra blankets, a tray of fresh toast and two mugs of hot chocolate. Grace pulled a blanket over her lap as Portia handed her a steaming mug, followed by a bowl of marshmallows.

'I picked them yesterday,' Portia said. 'They're fresh from the forest.'

Grace grabbed a handful, stuffed them in her mouth, then took another handful to sprinkle on her drink.

'Are you warming up a bit?' asked Portia.
'Or are you going to sneeze all over me, too?'

'I'm fine now we're away from *her royal snootiness*,' Grace said when she'd finished chewing.

'She does seem a bit uptight,' said Portia.

'I'm almost glad we're not playing troll-o tonight,' Grace grumbled. 'She doesn't deserve to see it. They're *supposed* to be enjoying *our* traditions too, not just telling us how good their stupid waterfolly is.'

'When we eventually get to play, I bet they'll love troll-o just as much as you do,' said Portia. 'I'm going to make sure they love dragons before they leave, too.'

'I can't *wait* till they're gone,' Grace groaned. 'I hate visitors, especially mean ones.'

'Me too,' Portia said, 'but maybe the

47

merfolk are just acting up because they're missing home? Think how we'd feel if we had to go all the way to the Outer Ocean.'

'Wet, probably,' Grace said sulkily.

Portia smiled. 'Cheer up. We might not be playing troll-o tonight, but at least that gives us time to have a look at the egg. What did you do with it?'

Grace's expression brightened. Keeping her blanket wrapped around her, she shuffled over to her bed and pulled back the covers. 'Ta-daa!'

The egg from the moat was tucked in a nest of pillows, covering them in a layer of moat slime.

'Crikey,' said Portia, coming over to join her.

Grace grinned. 'I know! There's no point pretending you don't approve, I can tell you're itching to study it.'

Portia grinned. 'Maybe – although I do hope its parents aren't worrying about it. We should definitely try and return it soon.'

'Fair enough. But perhaps we could sneak it into the royal baths first, see if it turns Queen Jeen's water purple? With any luck she might even leave early.'

Portia shook her head. 'There's no time for mucking about, Grace. Who knows what the adult dragons might do when they discover their egg is missing? Plus we can't have it hatching inside, Dad would freak out – not to mention Queen Jeen.'

Grace sighed. 'I guess you're right. But how are we going to get it back on the turret? I can't climb up now Dad's had the ivy removed. There's nothing to grab hold of.'

'We'll just have to find another way,' said Portia. She took Grace's blanket from her shoulders, wrapping the egg carefully inside. She handed the bundle to Grace, marched over to the door and held it open. 'Come on, let's start in the stables. I bet Bram can help.'

When the girls arrived in the stables, Bram Bramwell, the king's stable hand, had just finished feeding and grooming all the royal unicorns. The young imp put down his brush and greeted his friends.

'What do you think?' he said. 'Can you tell they spent the whole morning charging round the troll-o pitch?'

Portia wrapped her arms around Sprinkles's thick neck. 'Look at his lovely, foamy tail! They all look immaculate, Bram.'

'Apart from Poop,' Grace said, laughing at the state of her grubby unicorn.

No amount of grooming could make Poop look good. His fur was the colour of dirty dishwater, and he was constantly surrounded by flies. She gave him a tickle on the chin. He responded with a grumpy snort and a loud fart. Grace caught a brief whiff of roses, then clamped her fingers firmly over her nose. Portia was too late.

'Ugh, there it is,' she said, wafting a hand

in front of her face as the smell turned distinctly sour. 'Rotten eggs! Honestly, unicorns might look nice, but they're absolute stinkers!'

'Especially Poop,' Grace said. 'Have you not tried giving him witch wax? That normally helps the pong.'

'He wouldn't take it,' Bram said, taking off

his apron and hanging it on a peg. 'He's in a bad mood because I put ribbons in his mane.'

'I don't see any ribbons?' Grace said, puzzled.

Bram laughed. 'He ate them. D'you fancy coming to the tree house? I've got the rest of the day off now the troll-o's been postponed.'

'The tree house sounds great, but we've got something important to do,' Portia said, unwrapping the egg.

'Whoa!' said Bram, the tips of his pointy ears turning pink. 'Is that what I think it is?'

'I found it in the moat,' Grace explained. 'It's why the water was purple.'

'Dad would love to see that,' Bram said. 'He's crazy about magical creatures.'

'I'd love to show it to Bunkum, but we need to get it back in its nest,' Portia said.

'It's pretty urgent, actually,' Grace said. 'We wondered if you might be able to help us. Maybe you could turn yourself into something that can help us reach the turret?'

The imp grinned. 'Piece of cake,' he said. 'Speaking of which …' He clapped his hands and turned into … a giant sandwich. 'Oops. I was going for a slice of fruit loaf.'

Grace groaned. 'Very funny, but baked goods aren't really going to help on this occasion. You'll have to turn into something else, and you'll have to do it outside – oh, and we need to make sure no one sees us.'

CLAP! Bram turned back to his usual self again. 'No problem, we'll use the back door. Follow me. We'll soon have this egg back where it belongs.'

6

CHICKENS
DO NOT FLY

The sun was beginning to set as they made
their way outside. One by one, the castle's
shutters were closed, candles were lit behind
them and suit upon suit of armour was put
away with a distant clang. Grace had the
feeling the castle was slipping into its
pyjamas for the night. Up in their nests, the
dragons yawned and stretched, tucking their

wings around their young as they settled down to sleep.

'We'd better be quick,' Grace said. 'If anyone sees what we're up to, we'll be in big trouble.'

'I'm on it,' Bram said, turning himself into a catapult with a **CLAP!**

'Great idea,' Grace said, impressed. She carefully tucked the egg into Bram's sling and stretched it back. 'This ought to do the trick.'

'Are you sure about this?' Portia asked. 'What if you aim wrong and smash the egg?'

'Aim wrong? Pah! I'm the best shot in all Wondermere,' Grace said confidently, poking her tongue out and squinting as she lined up the sling with the nest. 'Ready, aim ... whoa there!'

The egg tumbled out of the sling and began rolling down the grassy bank towards the moat.

'It's going to fall in the water again!' Portia said, lifting her skirts and running after it.

Grace could run faster in her trousers. She just managed to stop the egg before it reached the moat. 'Oh, no you don't,' she said. 'Let's try again.'

'The sooner the better,' the catapult said. 'If you ask me that egg's got a mind of its own. I reckon it could hatch any time.'

Portia gave an anxious squeak, but Grace ignored her. 'Come on, egg, it's home time.' Again, she loaded the sling. Again, the egg seemed to have different plans. It hopped, skipped and *jumped* towards the moat. Grace couldn't keep up this time. The egg splashed into the moat, glowing purple and bubbling like before.

'Quick!' Portia said. 'Grab it before the whole moat changes colour again!'

Grace was in the water before her sister could finish her sentence. Seconds later, the egg was safely back in Portia's arms, and Grace was dripping wet on the bank beside her. 'This isn't going to work,' she said, wringing out her hair.

There was another **CLAP** as Bram turned back into his impish self. 'That egg is super lively,' he said. 'We need a Plan B.'

'You could turn into a bird and fly the egg up there?' Grace suggested.

'Good idea.' Bram gave a **CLAP**... and turned into a chicken.

'I meant a bird that can *fly*,' Grace said.

'Sorry,' Bram clucked, 'this is the only bird I can do.'

'You did your best,' Portia said kindly, 'and if we ever need an emergency chicken, we know exactly where to come.'

'We need a Plan C,' Grace groaned. 'Got any other bright ideas?'

The chicken cocked its head to one side. 'You could whack it up there with your troll-o mallet?' it said.

'No whacking!' Portia said, wrapping her arms around the egg protectively.

Grace paced up and down, thinking aloud.

'We could ask a giant to lift it back up?'

Portia shook her head. 'Giants are clumsy, plus they're extremely shy and hard to find.'

'We could ask the knights to form a human tower?' the chicken said, spreading its wings wide.

'No way, feather-brain,' said Portia. 'We can't involve anyone else. Dad'll go nuts if they tell him what we're up to.'

Grace's face lit up. 'We could use explosive swamp gas and blast it up there, like a firework?' Portia glared at her. 'OK, maybe not.'

'We have to do *something*,' Portia said as the egg wriggled in her arms. 'I swear this thing's desperate to get into the moat!'

Grace put a hand on the shell and smiled as she felt it pulsing steadily beneath her palm. 'I guess it likes being in the water,' she said.

There was a flurry of feathers as Bram turned back to normal. 'Well, I'm afraid I'm all out of ideas, and I need to get home before Dad starts to wonder where I am. Whatever you end up doing with that egg, you should probably keep it away from the moat.'

'You're right,' Portia said tiredly. 'We need to think again.'

'Thanks for your help, Bram,' Grace said with a yawn. 'I'm sure we'll have it sorted by the morning. Come on, Portia, let's take it back to our room for now. At least it can't upset Queen Jeen while it's safely indoors ...'

7

DO NOT WARM
A BROKEN EGG

Seeing as Grace was wearing trousers, the
girls smuggled the egg back into the castle
the same way they'd smuggled it out –
underneath Portia's enormous skirts.

'It won't stop wriggling,' she said as she
shuffled along the candlelit corridors. 'Eeee!
It tickles!'

'*Shhh*, someone will hear!' Grace said,

checking to make sure no one was near. 'Stand still a minute, let me take a look.' She crouched down and lifted a corner of Portia's petticoats. 'You know that tiny crack the bubbles were coming out of before? I think it's got bigger.'

'Oh, no,' said Portia, her voice high with panic. 'Maybe it broke when it rolled down the bank just now? Eeeee, it's so tickly!'

'Someone's coming!' Grace said, covering the egg again and leaping to her feet.

King Wonder came striding around the corner in his pyjamas and robe. Taffy Trafalgar was bounding along at his side, carrying several scrolls of parchment. 'Girls!' said their father. 'It's always lovely to see you, but shouldn't you be in bed by now?'

'**EEEEEE!**' said Portia.

King Wonder gave her a concerned look.

'Overtired,' said Taffy, peering at her over the top of his glasses. '*Stay up late, harm your fate,*' he quoted.

'Quite right, Taffy,' said the king. 'Off to bed at once. I want you both up bright and early tomorrow, ready to make a good impression on our guests.'

'That's exactly where we're heading, Dad,' said Grace. 'Come on, Portia ...'

'**TOO LATE!**' Portia cried, her eyes wide with panic.

'Exactly,' said her father, 'it's far too late.'

Now it was Portia's turn to wriggle. A wisp of purple smoke was beginning to pool around her ankles. 'Get rid of them,' she hissed at Grace, 'quick!'

'I beg your pardon?' said the king.

'She means those scrolls, Dad, not you and Taffy. Get rid of those scrolls, stop working so hard and go get a good night's sleep yourselves. Off you go,' Grace said, shooing them along.

Her father shook his head. 'You two really are a right royal pair of wonders. Come along, Taffy, these scrolls won't file themselves.'

No sooner than they'd disappeared round
the corner, Portia's skirts began to glow,
bathing the passageway in purple light.

'What now?!' Portia squealed, lifting her
skirts.

The egg started to roll wonkily off down the
corridor. Grace grabbed it and held it tight.
The crack in the shell grew bigger. The crack
grew longer. The crack grew wider. The crack

became *two* cracks,
then three, then four.
Finally the shell
shattered, and the
girls found
themselves lost in a
cloud of purple
smoke.

'You broke it!' Portia
spluttered, wafting the smoke away with
both hands.

'No I didn't,' Grace said. 'It hatched!'

The smoke cleared. A plump, purple baby
dragon sat in Grace's outstretched hands. It
gazed up at Grace, eyes wide. **'MEEP!'** it said,
licking her on the nose. It nuzzled into her
neck and started to purr.

'Aww!' said Grace. 'I think it's a boy!'

'And *I* think we're in big trouble,' Portia said. 'Imagine what Queen Jeen will do if she catches a dragon *inside* the castle!'

Grace pretended not to hear. She lifted the dragon up to her face to get a better look. 'He thinks I'm his mum! How about that? A pet dragon! I think I'll call you … Dennis. Welcome to your new home, Dennis!'

Portia shook her head.

'No way! We're not keeping him. Queen Jeen isn't the only one we have to worry about. What about its parents?'

'*His* parents,' Grace corrected her. 'You don't need dragon parents, do you, Dennis? Me and Portia can be your mummies!'

'**MEEP!**' Dennis made a leap for Portia, flapping his wings and falling flat on the floor. His bottom lip trembled.

'Aww, don't cry, little fella,' Grace said, picking him up and bundling him into Portia's arms. 'See? Mummy Portia loves you just as much as Mummy Grace.'

Dennis rubbed his nubbin of a beak against Portia's nose. 'He *is* kind of cute,' Portia said. 'Perhaps we could keep him for a *little* while ...'

'Did you hear that, Dennis? You can stay!'

'... Not for long! We need to get him back to his nest as soon as we can – but it's too risky while the merfolk are here. We'll have to keep him locked in our room until they leave, and the sooner we get him there, the better. We can't let anyone see him. Here, you hold him. I'll clear up the broken shell.'

Portia went to pass Dennis to Grace, but he wagged his little tail and a spout of purple flame shot from his mouth. Both girls were taken by surprise – Grace took a leap backwards in shock and Portia dropped him. Before they could stop him, he'd waddled off down the corridor, hiccuping and breathing out fire.

'Uh-oh,' Grace said, setting off after him. 'I guess bed will have to wait.'

'We have to catch him,' Portia said, running after her. 'He could burn the whole place down!'

'Relax,' Grace said, 'we'll catch him. Anyway, how much damage can one tiny dragon do?'

8

ALWAYS BASH
YOUR WAFFLES

The girls didn't get to bed at all that night.
Dennis led them all over Wondermere Castle
while its other inhabitants slept.

Along candlelit corridors, up spiralling
stone staircases, down into the dark
dungeons – wherever Dennis went, the girls
followed. But every time they came close
to catching him, Dennis either waddled

out of reach or shot out flames.

The sun was just beginning to rise when, at last, they cornered him inside the armour store. Grace made a lunge for him, but he dodged past both girls, knocking over a whole rack of mallets before scampering off down the corridor.

The noise woke Taffy Trafalgar, whose bedchamber was opposite the storeroom. The old troll appeared in his doorway, half asleep and dribbling, just as Dennis shot past.

The girls stopped in their tracks. 'Er ...' Portia said, 'we can explain ...'

Taffy smacked his lips together and muttered, 'Well done, Taffy, it's a golden star for you.'

Grace gave a sigh of relief. 'He's

sleepwalking,' she said, nudging him gently back into his room. 'Go back to bed, Taffy, nighty-night.'

They closed the door behind him and hurried off after Dennis, but the little dragon was nowhere in sight.

'I think he went into the Great Hall,' Grace said, leading the way. The room felt huge and cavernous in the dark.

'It's hopeless,' Portia said, her voice echoing off the walls.

A fire was burning low in the hall's enormous fireplace. Seeking comfort, Grace traipsed over to it, leaning heavily against the huge mantelpiece. 'We mustn't give up hope,' she said.

'But the castle's enormous and I'm worn out,' Portia said, collapsing into a chair.

'MEEP!'

'Did you hear that?' said Grace. Portia shook her head. 'Come here and put your ear against the wall ...'

Portia joined her sister. 'I can hear something scrabbling about!'

'He must've gone up the chimney,' said Grace, perking up.

Portia groaned. 'But the castle has *hundreds* of chimneys, and they're all connected. He could pop out in any fireplace, in any room. We can't possibly search them all!'

Grace sighed heavily. 'We'll have to – and fast. It's almost morning, we have to find him before someone else does.'

'But *how*?'

As if in answer, there was a distant clatter of pots and pans. 'He's popped out in the kitchens!' said Grace. She dashed off, dragging her exhausted sister behind her.

The serving trolls were clearly already up and about, though they were nowhere to be seen. The remains of their early breakfast were laid out on the enormous kitchen table, but Dennis wasn't interested in tea and toast. He was sitting – still, at last – in the middle of a pot of simmering water that hung in the kitchen's huge hearth. The pot's bottom was being tickled by the flames, but the heat didn't seem to bother Dennis at all. He splashed playfully around, turning the water purple. **'MEEP!'**

'There you are, you little rascal!' said Grace, going to give him a pat. 'Ow!'

'I *told you* he was dangerous,' said Portia, taking a seat at the table.

'He didn't bite me,' Grace said. 'Dennis loves me, don't you, Dennis? The pot's really hot, that's all. I'm surprised he can sit in it.'

Portia poured out two cups of tea and helped herself to a slice of cold toast. 'Of course!' she said, feeling a little more awake with every mouthful. 'Dragons like warmth – that's why they nest on the turrets. The heat rises up the chimneys and keeps the rooftops nice and toasty.'

'Speaking of toasty …' Grace said, helping herself to a slice. She dropped it instantly as a voice boomed out behind her.

'Girls! It makes a nice change to see you up and about so early!' Their father had appeared in the kitchen's wide arched doorway, wearing his velvet robe and slippers.

Quick as a flash, Grace grabbed the pan's heavy iron lid and went to put it over Dennis. But the little dragon was no longer in the pan. She shot Portia a panicked look and whispered, *'Gone!'*

'What's gone?' said King Wonder, pouring himself a cup of tea.

'Er, the tea,' Portia said, 'that's the last of it.'

'What are you doing in the kitchen anyway?' Grace blurted, too tired to be polite. 'Don't you normally have breakfast in bed?'

Their father rolled his eyes. 'Can't a king change his routine every once in a while?'

A flurry of soot fell from the chimney, followed by a muffled, **'MEEP!'**

The king cocked an ear towards the enormous fireplace. 'I beg your pardon?'

'Er, *me pleased* to see you?' Grace said, spreading her arms out wide in an effort to hide any sudden appearance from Dennis.

Portia got to her feet and forced the half-empty toast rack into her father's hands.

'Here you go, one breakfast, fit for a king. Go eat it in bed, relax for a little while longer.' She spun him around and started shooing him towards the kitchen door.

'If you insist,' said the king, heading into the corridor. 'It's a big day, with our guests here and all ...'

'Absolutely,' Portia said, pushing him out of the room, 'we'll ask one of the serving trolls to bring you a fresh pot of tea.'

CLANG!

Grace froze in horror as Dennis plopped out of the chimney and collided with the pot, spilling hot water over the flames with a **HISSSSS!** She leaped away just in time to avoid getting splashed. Then she watched, aghast, as the little dragon blinked, scrambled to his feet and started waddling after her father. **'MEEP!'**

'What was that?!' said the king, sticking his head back around the kitchen door.

Grace grabbed a saucepan from the pot rack and dropped it neatly over Dennis.

'*Me planning* on making waffles,' she said, bringing a booted foot heavily down on top of the pan to keep it from moving.

The king eyed her suspiciously. 'What are you up to?'

Portia looked desperately at her sister.

'It's an old trick Cook taught me,' Grace said, giving the pan a stomp for good measure. 'A bashed pan makes better waffles!'

'And spilled water helps too, I suppose?' the king said, looking at the mess.

'Deffo.' Grace was only glad the water was no longer purple.

'They're going to be some pretty amazing waffles,' said Portia, spinning their bewildered father back towards the door again. 'Now go and enjoy your breakfast before it gets even colder.'

The king refused to budge. 'Perhaps you could make some of these amazing waffles for our guests?'

'That's exactly why we're up so early,' Grace said. 'This first batch is for Queen Jeen herself.'

The saucepan began to edge along the floor. Grace quickly sat down on top of it.

The king looked astonished. '*Really?*'

'Really. I think maybe she and I got off on the wrong foot,' Grace said, grimacing as the pan thumped and bumped beneath her. 'What with all that stuff about troll-o

being better than waterfolly and me sneezing

on her and everything.'

'MEEP!'

'*Me probably* better mix the batter,' Portia

said. 'That pan sounds ready to go!'

King Wonder shook his head. 'I'm not sure

getting up early agrees with you two, and I'm

not sure Queen Jeen would appreciate waffles from a pan that's been dragged all over the floor, either. But I do admire the sentiment. Carry on.'

He'd just turned his back when Dennis managed to overturn the pan. Grace sprawled on to the floor and Dennis scurried under the table, where he hiccuped out a fresh spout of flame, setting fire to the tablecloth.

King Wonder turned on his heel and sniffed the air. 'Something's burning,' he said. 'Get a move on, those merfolk will already be up and training ...'

'MEEP!'

'... And *do* try and speak properly.'

'*Me promise,*' Grace said exhaustedly as the king finally left the room. 'Just our luck – now we have to make breakfast as well as babysit the realm's naughtiest dragon.'

'Making breakfast might have to wait,' said Portia, putting out the smouldering tablecloth with the last dribble of tea from the pot.

'How'd you figure that?' Grace said, dusting herself down.

'Because we're rubbish babysitters,' Portia groaned. 'Dennis is off again!'

Grace spun around just in time to see Dennis's tail disappearing as he bounded gleefully out of the kitchen.

9

ALWAYS LOCK
THE BATHROOM DOOR

The whole castle was waking up. Grace had
to dodge serving trolls as they bustled about,
carrying breakfast trays and baskets of
firewood. One was busy sweeping up the
pieces of spotted eggshell. Another was
swishing a feather duster at a tell-tale wisp
of purple smoke that lingered in the corridor.
But there was no sign of Dennis.

'I swear he's getting faster,' Grace complained, weaving her way round the grumbling troll.

'At least he isn't flying yet,' Portia said quietly. 'He'll be even harder to catch then. You do realise he's heading straight towards the baths? I hope we catch him before—'

A terrified scream filled the air.

'Too late!' Grace said, forcing her exhausted legs back into a run.

It seemed Sir Arthur and Sir Oliver had heard the commotion, too. They reached the baths at the same time as the girls and stepped in front of them to block the way. 'Halt, princesses,' said Sir Oliver, holding out an outstretched palm. 'Whatever is causing this commotion could be d-d-dangerous!'

'Not as dangerous as *I* will be if you don't move out of my way,' Grace said, glaring at the boys.

They stepped aside, clutching one another for comfort. Grace and Portia strode boldly past them into the baths, just as another deafening scream rang out. Sir Arthur whimpered. 'P-perhaps Princess Grace's legendary good luck will keep them safe?'

The girls used the royal baths every day to clean up after troll-o practice, so Grace was prepared for the rush of steam – but she wasn't prepared for it to be *purple*.

'Uh-oh,' she said, following the sounds of shrieking and frantic splashing to the main bath. It was a huge oval-shaped pool, surrounded by ornate pillars and shallow steps that led down into the water.

The bath was normally a delicate turquoise, turning to emerald green in its deep centre. But not today. Today, the whole thing was purple, and filled with very unhappy merfolk.

'**HELP!**' cried Marlin, his tail churning the water in panic.

Brooke sped past him, wailing, 'I want to go home!'

Queen Jeen spotted the girls and waved her arms at them, her face full of panic. 'There's a dragon in the bath!' she shrieked.

All the noise had not escaped King Wonder's attention. 'A dragon?' he said, striding up behind Grace and Portia. 'You must be mistaken, your highness!'

Taffy Trafalgar bumbled up to join them. 'Fret not, your royal wetness,' he said, peering blindly at the pool through his

steamed-up glasses, 'there are no dragons inside Wondermere Castle!'

'Er,' said Grace, 'there might just be one *tiny* one, actually ...'

As if on cue, Dennis bobbed up in the middle of the pool. He began floating on his back, wings flapping lazily and turning him in slow circles.

'What in all Wonder ... ?!' said the king.

Dennis wagged his little tail in the water and a stream of bubbles shot out of his bottom. **'MEEP!'** he cried happily.

'Revolting!' Queen Jeen spat.

'He's just doing what babies do,' Grace said, wading into the water fully clothed to retrieve Dennis.

'He's a menace!' the queen said, balling her fists in fury.

Dennis began turning gleeful cartwheels in the water. The bath glowed purple, churning and frothing as Dennis played and Queen Jeen and her entourage continued to flap about hysterically.

'We need clean water, clear visibility and space to stretch our fins,' she complained. 'How are we supposed to train and play with *vermin* in the water?! Honestly! I've never been so insulted!'

'Please accept my most sincere apologies,' said King Wonder from the poolside. 'I assure you nothing like this has ever happened before. Grace, what have you got to say for yourself?'

Grace had finally got hold of Dennis. Worn out from his all-night adventure, he allowed her to scoop him into her arms.

He promptly fell asleep and started snoring. 'Sorry, Dad,' she said, 'but can you pass me a net or something? Dennis just did a *you-know-what* in the water.'

'It's an outrage!' Queen Jeen said.

Grace waded back towards her sister, gripping Dennis tightly under one arm as Portia gave her a hand out of the water. 'I'm sorry Dennis gave you a shock, your majesty,' she said, turning back to face Queen Jeen. 'It won't happen again.'

'It most certainly won't, because we're leaving.' Queen Jeen began ushering her people out of the water towards their chariots, which were lined up, semi-submerged, along the pool's steps.

'Please don't leave,' King Wonder said, 'just let me deal with this ... problem.' He scowled at Grace. *Dennis?*

'We found him in the moat,' Portia gushed. 'Well, his egg anyway. It's what turned it purple! Fascinating, really, no one's ever considered a dragon's effect on water before. We certainly didn't know he was going to hatch.'

'We tried putting him straight back on the turrets,' Grace explained, 'but we couldn't reach, which is all your fault really, seeing as you had the ivy stripped off ...'

The king looked even grumpier than Poop after a hard game of troll-o. Grace gave Portia a desperate look.

Portia addressed the merqueen. 'We're really sorry he upset you, Queen Jeen – honestly,' she said, 'but he didn't mean to. He's just a baby.'

'He's really cute once you get to know him,' Grace said, holding Dennis up so the merqueen might get a better look. 'See?'

Dennis blew a raspberry in his sleep. The king's face softened a little, but Queen Jeen looked horrified. 'Cute?' she squealed, backing away. 'That thing nearly killed me!'

Grace was tired, hungry and her patience had run out. 'Nearly killed you?! You really are a great, wet—'

Before she could say '*wimp*', Portia

clamped a hand over her mouth. 'What Grace would like to say is that you really are a great, wet wonder. You have such fighting spirit, something we knights really value. We're so looking forward to seeing you and your squad at your best, playing waterfolly. Isn't that right, Grace?'

She gave Grace a stern look before releasing her hand from her mouth.

'That's right,' Grace fibbed. 'It's your exhibition game tomorrow, isn't it? Can't wait. We'll be watching from the drawbridge, best view of the moat.'

The merqueen lifted her chin and folded her arms across her chest. 'Actually, I think we'll showcase our sport *tonight*.'

'But it's the *troll-o* tonight!' Grace said.

King Wonder shook his head. 'The troll-o

can wait another day. What matters most is that our guests feel happy and comfortable.'

The merqueen narrowed her eyes. 'We'll only be *happy and comfortable* once that revolting creature is gone.'

'Dennis is going, don't worry,' Portia said, smiling her sweetest smile.

'He most certainly is,' said her father. 'You two will take that dragon far away from Wondermere Castle *at once.*'

'Far away?!' Grace said, holding Dennis a little tighter.

'Far, *far* away,' the king repeated angrily, drawing himself up to his full height. 'He can return once our guests are safely back at the Outer Ocean, reflecting on a long and happy visit to Wondermere.'

'But a baby dragon needs to be close to its

parents ...' Portia began, but King Wonder raised his voice.

'ENOUGH,' he yelled. 'I don't want to hear another peep out of either of you – *or* your dragon! Now get that thing out of here before I banish you as well!'

10

DO NOT SIT ON A POP-WEASEL

The girls took Dennis straight to the stables.

'Aww, he's adorable,' Bram said.

'I know, right?' said Grace, gazing lovingly at Dennis, who was still fast asleep in her arms. 'How could anyone not want him around?'

'To be fair, I'm not sure *I'd* want to

share a bath with someone who used it as a toilet,' Portia said.

Grace sighed. 'Dad says we have to take him far, far away. We were wondering – d'you think your dad might look after him? It's only for a few days while the merfolk are here.'

'If Bunkum doesn't mind … ?' Portia added.

'Mind?!' Bram chuckled. 'He'll be chuffed to bits. Although our tree house isn't exactly *far, far away …*'

'Dad doesn't need to know,' Grace said, settling Dennis into a bed of hay, 'and best of all, we can come and visit, every day.'

The girls dashed off to put on their armour while Bram saddled the unicorns. Dennis stayed asleep while Grace wrapped him in

the folds of her cloak and carefully mounted
Poop.

'Say hi to Dad from me,' Bram said,
waving them off. 'I'll be along later, once I've
finished work!'

The journey was a fairly short and very
familiar one: out the back door of the royal
stables, over the little stone bridge and into
the enchanted depths of Wondermere Forest.

Grace barely noticed the sunlight warming
her armour as Poop picked his way grouchily
through whole villages of fairy toadstools,
past clusters of goblin burrows and through
patches of bristly bog brambles. At one point
Poop stopped to poke his tongue out at a
leprechaun, but Grace didn't even notice, let
alone try to stop him.

Her mind was whirling. She was disgusted

with Queen Jeen and absolutely furious with her father. 'I can't believe he took her side!' she complained as they arrived at the Bramwells' tree house.

'He didn't have much choice,' said Portia reasonably. 'We're supposed to be *strengthening* relations with the Outer Ocean, not making them worse.'

'I know,' Grace said sadly, slipping out of her saddle.

The hum of mumblebees filled the air. They bumbled busily around the marshmallows that grew on the branches of the imps' tree house. Poop and Sprinkles began to graze happily, nibbling at the low-hanging sweets and gobbling up any that had fallen on the ground. Wild at heart, the unicorns were at their happiest among the trees. Grace knew they wouldn't stray. Like her, they could happily stay here forever.

The imps' tree house was her favourite place in all Wondermere. It was always warm and welcoming, nestled in the heart of the forest, and every last bit of it wrapped in sparkling twinkle lights. Even Bunkum's prized pile of magical manure had its own unique appeal, glittering in the dappled light and smelling more like cake than dung.

Just being here was making Grace feel a little bit better. Having Dennis snuggled on her shoulder helped, too.

He was starting to stir as the girls climbed the tree house's rickety wooden steps and knocked on the door. 'Try not to worry,' Portia said. 'I'm sure Bunkum will keep Dennis safe until we can get him back in his

nest. Anyway, I'm sure
Dad would never *really*
let anything bad
happen to a cute little
baby dragon.'

'Did somebody say
cute little baby dragon?'
The tree-house door was
flung open by an old imp in a leather apron.
Bunkum Bramwell took one look at Dennis
and – **POP!** – turned himself
into a giant magnifying
glass. 'Let me get a
closer look!'

'His name's Dennis,'
Grace said proudly. 'You
can hold him, if you like?
I think he's waking up.'

POP! Bunkum turned himself back to normal, took Dennis gently in his arms and ushered the girls inside.

The tree-house kitchen was snug and cosy. Portia settled into her usual chair at the little table, which Grace leaned tiredly against.

'I'm very glad to see you both,' Bunkum said, 'and it's lovely to meet your new friend, too. What a lot of excitement for one day, especially with the troll-o to look forward to this evening.'

'It's been postponed again,' Portia explained. 'Queen Jeen is insisting they play their waterfolly showcase tonight instead.'

'Oh, well. That'll be quite a spectacle too. I've been to the coast before and seen them play with my own eyes, it's really quite exhilarating.'

'If you say so,' Grace huffed. She went to take a seat at the table, but the seat toppled out of her reach.

Bunkum chuckled. 'Looks like Wesley's glad to see you, too!'

'Wesley?' Grace said, looking around for signs of the Bramwells' beloved pet pop-weasel, who was extremely shy and also invisible. 'Where is he?'

'By your feet,' said Bunkum, pointing at the floor.

Grace picked a spot by her armoured toes and waved at it. 'Hey, Wesley.'

Dennis seemed to have no trouble spotting him. He clambered out of Bunkum's arms, *meep*ing happily and tumbling around Grace's feet with his new see-through friend.

Bunkum turned his attention to the girls.

'I can't help but notice that *you two* aren't as happy as *those two*,' he said. 'How about I make us some hot chocolate, and you can tell me why this merqueen's bothering you so much?'

Grace was more than happy to let Portia do the talking. It left her mouth free for cookies and hot chocolate. She was soon feeling a lot more cheerful.

'I *hate* Queen Jeen,' she said, dunking a seventh biscuit into her third drink.

'No, you don't,' Bunkum said gently, 'and Queen Jeen doesn't *hate* dragons. She just doesn't understand them, that's all. We're not all lucky enough to spend time with magical creatures,' he said, looking fondly at a space Grace suspected contained Wesley.

'I expect life's very different in the Outer Ocean,' Portia agreed.

'Absolutely, princess,' Bunkum continued. 'I'm sure the merqueen will *love* Dennis once she gets to know him. You two might even come to like *her* once you've spent a bit more time together.'

Grace scowled. 'Not a chance.' She was beginning to feel drowsy in the warmth of the tree house. She made a pillow with her hands and laid her head on the table, watching sleepily as Bunkum bustled about the kitchen. Her eyelids began to droop as he went to the window and tugged on a rope, raising a bucket of well water from outside. He poured it into the sink ready to do the washing-up.

'Look!' Portia said, giving Grace a shake. 'So cute!'

Dennis climbed up Bunkum's leg and clambered into the sink, wedging himself into the wooden washing-up bowl. The soap suds turned purple as he sank down with a dopey grin on his face. **'MEEP!'**

'He loves water,' Grace said, stifling a yawn, 'scaly little weirdo.'

'It's certainly unusual behaviour for a dragon,' Bunkum said. 'You'd think he'd be busy trying to fly out of the window. Still, he'll be flying rings around you before you know it. Get some rest while you still can!'

'Rest would be nice,' Portia admitted.

Bunkum smiled. 'You two head up to the spare room and get some sleep. I'll happily keep an eye on this little rascal.'

The girls gave their friend a grateful smile and trudged tiredly up to their waiting bunks.

11

DO NOT FALL ASLEEP IN YOUR ARMOUR

Grace woke to the sound of giggling. She rubbed her eyes and looked across to Portia's bunk. It was empty and the covers had been neatly tucked in. Her sister's laughter carried up the stairs, accompanied by Bunkum's. There was a flurry of happy *meep*ing, then she heard Bram's voice, too.

He must be back from the stables, Grace

thought. *How long have I been asleep?*

She'd been so tired she'd gone to bed in her armour. She tugged it off now, swinging her arms back and stretching to ease her stiff joints, then headed downstairs.

The kitchen looked even more welcoming in the twilight. Grace gave Bram a little wave. Dennis, who'd been enjoying a tickle on Bram's lap, scurried over to Grace as soon as he saw her, bumping his head against her ankles. **'MEEP!'**

'Steady on, Dennis,' she said, bending down to pet him.

Bunkum handed her a mug of sweet nettle soup. 'You've been out like a light all day,' he said. 'I'm not surprised after this rascal ran you both ragged.'

'I only just woke up, too,' Portia said

between sips of soup. 'Bram's taught
Dennis to fetch – show her, Bram!'

'It only works if I throw it in the
sink,' Bram said, grabbing a wooden
spoon and tossing it into the full
washing-up bowl. 'Go fetch,
Dennis!'

Dennis dashed after
the spoon, claws
slipping comically on
the kitchen floor.

He tugged
himself up to

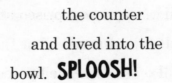

the counter
and dived into the
bowl. **SPLOOSH!**

'Brilliant,' Grace said, taking a seat at the table. 'Dennis is the best pet ever.'

Portia sighed. 'You know we can't keep him. He belongs in his nest.'

'I s'pose,' Grace huffed.

'I agree,' Bunkum said. 'He'll be able to fly himself up to his nest soon enough. He just needs someone to show him how.'

Portia's face brightened. 'Of course! Dennis hasn't started flying yet because he hasn't had his parents around to teach him!'

'MEEP!' said Dennis, merrily spitting a jet of purple water at Grace.

'But right now *we're* his parents,' Grace said, drying her face on a patchwork tea towel. 'How are we supposed to teach him? We can't fly.'

Portia shrugged, but Bunkum gave them a smile. 'I'm sure you'll figure something out. The longer Dennis stays away from his own kind, the harder it'll be for him to live a normal life.'

Grace sighed. 'You're right. We have to get him flying.'

'Definitely,' Bram said. 'Then he can go back to his nest without Queen Jeen even batting an eye. Once he's up on the turrets no one will be able to tell him apart from the other dragons.

'But *we'll* know him,' said Portia, 'and we'll still get to watch him grow up, like a normal dragon should.'

'But Dennis isn't a normal dragon,' Grace said, 'he's special.'

'MEEP!' said Dennis, bringing her the wooden spoon. He dropped it at her feet and wagged his little tail, ready to play again.

Portia finished her soup and gave Grace's shoulder a squeeze. 'He *is* special – that's why we need to take the very best care of him. He needs his nest, the sooner the better.'

'Your sister's right,' Bunkum agreed, topping up their soup mugs. 'It'll be good for him. He's just a baby. He ought to be with his parents.'

'If you're going to teach him to fly, you'd better hurry up,' Bram said. 'The waterfolly starts in a couple of hours. The whole realm will be watching, and Queen Jeen won't want to see Dennis anywhere other than in his nest.'

'Can you imagine how mad she'd be otherwise?' Portia said.

That did it. Grace finished her soup and wiped her mouth on her tunic sleeve. 'No *way* am I giving that misery guts an excuse to cancel troll-o for a *third* time. Come on, Dennis, your mummies are going to get you airborne!'

12

DO NOT DIVE
INTO DUNG

The girls had never given anyone a flying
lesson before, but the lower branches of the
marshmallow tree felt like a good place to
start.

Grace stood on the tree's lowest limb with
Dennis, while Portia and Bram waited below,
calling out encouragement.

'Come on, Dennis,' Portia said, holding out

her arms, 'you can do it!'

Dennis wriggled out of Grace's arms and
scrambled on to her back where she couldn't
reach him. 'I think he's scared,' she said,
feeling his little body tremble.

'You're only a few feet off the ground,'
Bram said. 'How's he going to cope with a
turret if he doesn't like heights?'

'He'll be grand,' Grace said, sounding more
confident than she felt. 'Let's just start with
him jumping off my shoulder, and maybe we
should find someplace with a softer landing.'

They tried encouraging Dennis to jump
into a pile of freshly raked marshmallows,
into a bed of candy-moss, and even into
Bunkum's glittering dung heap, but Dennis
was having none of it. The more they tried,
the more he dug his claws in, clinging to

Grace like his life
depended on it. 'MEEP!'

'Get down, Dennis!'
Grace said as Dennis
clambered on top of
her head, his eyes
round with panic. She
tried to remove him, but
the more she tugged,
the tighter he clung,
bouncing up and down
like a squeeze box.

'Nature's a curious thing,'
said Bunkum, who was
busy pouring chocolate
chips into all the wood-
nymph feeders

in the garden. 'He'll figure it out in his own sweet time. Bram, would you fetch me a bucket of well water? I need to fill the boggart bath.'

Bram filled the bucket, walking it steadily back across the garden, trying not to let it spill.

Grace was ready to give up. 'It's hopeless,' she said, the dragon still gripping her scalp as she trudged up the tree-house steps for a biscuit break. 'Dennis is going to have to stay banished. He isn't going to start flying any time soon.'

Just then, Bram passed underneath them with his full bucket. In a heartbeat, Dennis relaxed his grip on Grace and launched himself into the air, nosediving gleefully into the bucket. **SPLOP!**

Grace jumped down to the ground and danced around Bram's bucket. 'He did it! Dennis flew!'

'Er, he sort of *fell*, actually,' said Bram, putting the bucket down. It rocked and swayed as Dennis wriggled happily around. Portia and Bunkum both came to get a better look.

'He really does like water, doesn't he?' said Bunkum. Dennis dipped his nose beneath the surface and blew bubbles.

Portia took her notebook from her dress pocket and flipped through her observations. 'He's always trying to sit in water. I think maybe his egg spent too long in the moat ...'

'Maybe it damaged him?' Bram said quietly. 'Maybe he won't *ever* fly?'

Grace shook her head. 'Dennis isn't

damaged, he's perfect – and he's going to fly right up to that turret to show Queen *Mean* just how amazing dragons really are ...'

'I'm not so sure—' Portia began, but Grace interrupted her.

'... And when Dennis has put on a stunning aerial display, it'll be *our* turn to show those snooty mermaids our awesome skills on the troll-o pitch.' Grace punched the air with an armoured fist, and

raised her voice so the whole forest might hear. 'They think knights are thugs! They call our dragons vermin! They think they're so superior with their fancy waterfolly moves. So they can turn cartwheels underwater? Big deal! We'll show them just how graceful scales and armour can be – isn't that right, Dennis?'

There was a rumble from the bucket. A steady stream of purple bubbles floated up from Dennis's bottom. **'MEEP!'**

'That was a very rousing speech, Grace,' Bram said, 'but I still don't see any sign of him flying. Maybe you should stick to your first plan and leave Dennis here with us until the merfolk leave? That way you can just focus on enjoying the waterfolly tonight, and showing off your troll-o skills tomorrow.'

Grace shook her head. 'No way,' she said. 'I'm not going back to the castle without Dennis. The only way I'll enjoy watching the merfolk play is knowing Dennis is there, too.'

'I agree,' Portia said. 'It's a matter of principle.'

'Fair enough, but it's also a matter of heights and gravity and wing flapping,' Bram said.

'Actually, it sounds like a matter of *magic*,' Bunkum suggested, changing briefly into a signpost and pointing into the depths of the forest. 'I'll bet the local witch can help. Old Mother Merriwinkle's potions can fix pretty much anything.'

'Of course,' Portia said. 'She's helped us before, when Poop needed a makeover. At least she *tried* to help ...'

Grace looked at Poop's grubby mane and grimaced. 'To be fair, making Poop look smart was a pretty big ask.'

'If you're quick you might catch her before the market closes for the day,' Bram said, 'although she's been busy lately, training her granddaughter. Verity's a friend of mine, say hi if you see her.'

'Will do,' said Portia, mounting Sprinkles.

'Do you mind looking after Dennis while we're gone?' Grace said, swinging her leg over Poop's saddle.

'We'd be delighted to,' said Bunkum cheerfully.

Bram lifted Dennis gently out of the bucket. 'Does Dennis want to play fetch with Uncle Bram?'

The dragon wagged his tail and licked

him on the nose.

'LET'S DO THIS,' Grace said, giving Poop's reins a quick tug. 'Poop, carry on eating marshmallows – and whatever you do, *don't* take us to Mother Merriwinkle!'

Poop was delighted to disobey. Just as Grace expected, he stopped chewing and trotted off in the direction of the market.

13

DO NOT TRUST
A TRAINEE WITCH

Thanks to Poop stopping to sneer at boggarts, some of the stallholders were packing up by the time they reached the market square.

'I guess they're closing early so they can go and watch the waterfolly,' Portia said.

Grace tutted. 'I hope the witch hasn't already left.'

To Poop's delight, one of the stalls that was

still open was selling roasted hazel gums.
He was suddenly keen to walk much faster.
In fact, he walked right into the market,
trampling a farmer's stall and knocking
over her barrow of turnips.

'Sorry!' Grace said, hopping hurriedly out
of the saddle. She led Poop to the fountain in
the middle of the square, tied his reins to a
railing, then dashed off to buy some of the
gums.

Poop's ears twitched in anticipation as she
marched back, carrying a bulging paper bag
in each hand. She poured the treats into the
unicorns' nosebags. 'Please run away,' she
said firmly. 'I don't want to find you here
when we're done.'

Portia tied Sprinkles up beside him, then
the girls set about looking for the witch.

'I hope we haven't missed her,' Portia said
as they picked their way between tables and
barrows.

'Me too,' Grace said. She couldn't resist
glancing back over her shoulder at Poop. He
was standing stock still save for his lower
jaw, which was busy circling around a hazel
gum. He looked tremendously pleased with
himself.

'Can I interest you ladies in some beard
shampoo?' said a goblin, stepping out from
his stall and blocking their path. 'Choose
from essence of bogberries, pure pixie wort or
genuine frog flax. Each one is guaranteed to
give you a face full of luxuriant hair!'

'No thanks,' said Portia, trying to get
around him, 'we don't have beards.'

'But you *could* have!' the goblin said.

'It's very tempting, but we're in a hurry,' Grace said, tugging Portia with her as she dodged around him. 'Look, there's the witch's stall!'

A cauldron was bubbling gently away over hot embers. A knobbly three-legged table stood alongside it, its top cluttered with several jars, a variety of misshapen bottles and a huge spell book. Behind it all stood a stumpy hatstand, draped in a cloak with a witch's pointed hat dumped on top.

'No witch,' Portia said, disappointed.

'And what d'you think *I* am? A toadstool?!' A slender green arm shot out from beneath the hanging cloak and pushed up the hat's wide brim to reveal a moody young witch.

'Goodness,' said Portia. 'I thought you were a hatstand.'

'Charming,' said the witch.

Grace frowned. 'Where's Mother Merriwinkle? We need a proper witch.'

'I *am* a proper witch,' the young witch said snottily. 'Gran's left me in charge today. Verity Merriwinkle, at your service.'

'Nice to meet you, Verity,' said Portia, shaking the young witch's hand. 'I'm Portia Wonder and this is my sister, Grace. Bram sent us to see you, he says hi.'

'I know who you two are,' said Verity, looking pleased. 'I must've seen you play in about a thousand troll-o matches. So: are you going to buy something or what?'

Grace pulled her shoulders back. 'We need a flying potion,' she said.

'Is it for you?' Verity asked. 'Because only witches and magical creatures can fly,

136

even with potions involved.'

'It's for a dragon,' Portia said.

Verity wrinkled her crooked nose. 'Can't it fly already?'

Grace bristled. 'Not yet, and he needs to learn, fast. We need him in his nest before the waterfolly starts. Can you help us or not?'

Verity let out a long, low whistle. 'Dragons are pretty big. I don't know if I've got enough ingredients ...'

'He's only a baby,' Portia said. 'We don't need much, only we really are in a rush.'

'You're in luck,' Verity said, rolling up her sleeves and opening her grandmother's enormous spell book. 'It just so happens flying potions are my speciality.'

Grace watched as a newt scuttled out from between the book's dusty pages.

'Let's see,' Verity said, studying the list of contents. *Spell for Fangs, Spell for Flatulence* – aha! *Spell for Flight*, page six thousand and fifty-six.'

She flicked to the right page, ran a crooked green finger down the list of ingredients and began dumping the contents of various jars and bottles into her grandmother's cauldron. 'That ought to do it.'

Verity stirred the concoction with her wand, muttering incantations. The mixture turned a shocking shade of blue. 'Are you sure you're doing it right?' Grace said, reading the spell for herself. 'In the picture it's orange with blue stripes.'

'Is it?' said Verity. 'Oh, yeah … We could try following the instructions, I s'pose.'

Portia gave Grace an alarmed look while

Verity rummaged through her stock of ingredients. 'Hmm, no frog flax. I'll add webweed instead. It'll be fine. Probably.'

Verity went to pour in the webweed, but Grace stopped her. 'Hang on,' she said, 'I'm pretty sure that goblin was selling frog flax ...' She rushed off, returning quickly with a bottle of purple liquid.

Verity scanned the label. 'I guess we could add it. I don't see what harm it can do.'

'Right, it's going in,' Grace said, snatching the bottle back, taking out the stopper and glugging the whole lot into the cauldron. The mixture flashed, fizzed and then turned orange. 'There. *Now* it looks more like the picture.'

Verity pouted. 'No it doesn't, there are no stripes.'

Grace grinned triumphantly as a rack of blue stripes began to appear on the potion's surface. **'TA-DAAA!'**

'Beginner's luck,' Verity sniffed.

'They don't call me the luckiest girl in the kingdom for nothing,' Grace said with a shrug.

'I'm not sure luck has anything to do with it,' Portia said. 'Reading the instructions always helps. Are you *sure* you know what you're doing?'

Verity flinched. 'Do you honestly think my gran would've left me in charge if I didn't?' She gave the disgusting concoction one last stir, ladled it into an empty bottle and put a stopper in the neck. 'There. I reckon that should be enough for a small dragon.'

Portia looked unconvinced. 'And you're sure it's going to work?'

'I guess we'll soon find out,' Grace said, her chest swelling with pride. 'I made a potion!'

'*We* made a potion,' Verity corrected her, 'and I still need paying.'

'But Grace did most of the work!' Portia protested.

Verity ignored her. 'I take gold, gems or genuine promises. A good viewing spot for the waterfolly would be appreciated, too.'

'If your potion works you can join us on the drawbridge, but I doubt it'll be very entertaining,' Grace said.

She dug around in her pocket for a handful of coins, then handed them to Verity.

The witch handed over the bottle in return. 'Any nasty side effects, don't blame me.'

Portia grimaced, but Grace beamed. 'Let's go, Portia. I feel an epic quest coming on!'

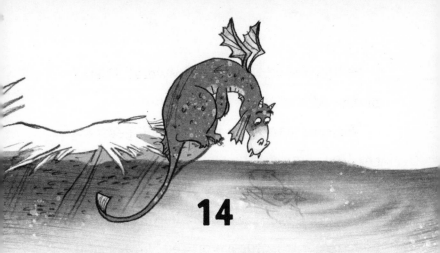

14

DO NOT TURN YOUR BACK
ON A GREEDY UNICORN

Grace and Portia couldn't wait to get back to
the tree house and try the potion on Dennis,
but the goblin stallholder had other ideas.

'How was the frog flax?' he said. 'Can I
interest you in some moustache wax to go
with it?' He waved another bottle at Grace as
she marched by.

'Sorry, can't stop,' she said, brushing past

him, 'but I'll be sure to recommend it to people who actually have facial hair.'

'Maybe a jar of toe jam instead?' he said, trailing them all the way to the fountain and their unicorns. 'Goes lovely on toast!'

'Thanks, but if you don't leave us alone I'll have to set my unicorn on you,' Grace said. Poop's face brightened. He lowered his long nose and glared at the goblin. The goblin hurried away, muttering something about having left the kettle on.

Grace opened her saddlebag to make room for the potion.

She only put the bottle down for a second, but that was all it took. Poop had spotted it. Before she could stop him, he bit off the stopper, upended the bottle and started guzzling it down.

'BAD UNICORN!' Grace said, snatching the bottle away.

'There's none left!' Portia wailed.

Poop belched, then he farted. Never mind a brief whiff of eggs and roses; this time his bottom fired out flames.

Portia shrieked, but Grace just stared as sparkling fire continued to shoot from Poop's rear end. 'For pixies' sake! You've done some stupid, greedy things in your time, matey-boy, but this really takes the biscuit!'

For once in his life Poop actually looked rather ashamed, but then – with one almighty **PARP!** – he shot into the sky.

'WHOA!' Grace hollered.

'I don't think *whoa*-ing will help,' said Portia seriously. 'He's going too fast to hear you.'

Verity ran over to join them, her black cloak flapping behind her. 'You never told me you had a flying unicorn?!'

'I don't,' Grace said, gazing up at Poop, who was whizzing around like a deflating balloon. 'I had a regular unicorn with a seriously bad attitude, until he swallowed that flying potion.'

'*I* made him fly?' Verity said.

'*We* made him fly,' Grace said. 'It was *my* idea to add the frog flax.'

'You didn't just make him *fly*,' Portia said, squinting up at Poop's flaming trail. 'You made him *fart*. Like, really, *really* fart.'

'Don't blame me,' Verity said. 'That potion was intended for a dragon, not a unicorn. To be honest I'm amazed it worked at all. I can't wait to tell Gran.'

Grace glared at her. 'I thought you said flying potions were your speciality?'

Verity shrugged. 'They are now. I suppose you'll be needing another batch for your dragon? Just say the word and I'll whip up some more, magical genius that I am.'

'Magical genius?!' Portia said. 'The potion only works because Grace added the frog flax!'

'And because I did the rest. If you're so good at making potions, do it yourself.' Verity turned on her heel and started storming back to her stall. 'Good luck finding a wand!'

'We can't do it without her,' Grace said to Portia. 'At least we know the potion works. It might work even better on Dennis.'

'I don't trust her,' said Portia. 'Who knows what effect that potion would have had if you hadn't corrected it? Poop might have exploded!'

BANG! Poop backfired, sending him zooming towards the clouds. Verity stopped in her tracks, looked up and started laughing. Grace burst out laughing too. Even Portia couldn't help joining in.

'It *is* sort of funny,'
Portia said, 'but we need him
back. How soon will the potion
wear off?'

'No idea,' Verity said. 'Could last all
day. Although he might come down faster if
we could make him a bit heavier ...'

Grace scoffed. 'He's just eaten a ton of
marshmallows and a bag of roasted hazel
gums, how much heavier can he get?'

Verity's face brightened. 'I could fly you up
to him on my broom!'

Grace frowned. 'Wait – you have a *flying broom*?'

'Of course I do, I'm a witch.'

'So you could just fly our baby dragon up to the castle turret, simple as anything?'

Portia shook her head. 'Dennis needs to learn how to use his wings before we leave him up there. What if he fell out of the nest?'

'Ouch,' said Verity.

'OK,' said Grace, 'so we *definitely* need more potion.'

'What we need is more *time*,' Portia said. 'The waterfolly starts in an hour, and we still need to make extra potion, fetch Dennis, get him flying *and* rescue Poop!'

'We can do this,' Grace said determinedly, 'but we'll have to split up. Verity, can you help me rescue Poop? We'll need to use your broom.'

'Make your mind up,' Verity said. 'I thought you wanted me to make more potion?'

Grace shook her head. 'Not enough time. Portia can brew it while we fetch Poop; she's seen how it's done. You'll just need to lend her your wand.'

'Fine,' Verity said, reluctantly handing it over, 'but be careful with it.'

'I will. And *I* won't forget to add the frog flax,' Portia said, making Verity scowl.

'Great,' Grace said. 'When you've made it, head straight to the tree house. Sprinkles has been fed, he'll be full of energy and ready to gallop. Grab Dennis and meet us at the castle. I just hope we can get there before the waterfolly starts ...'

'Of course we can,' said Portia. She gave Grace a high five, then hurried off to find the goblin, calling over her shoulder, 'You're the luckiest girl in the kingdom!'

'I really hope that's true,' Grace said. 'Verity, fetch your broom – and make it snappy. We're going to get my unicorn back.'

15

DO NOT DISTRACT
THE DRIVER

'Hop on, princess,' said Verity, straddling her
broomstick.

Grace took a seat behind her. 'Can you
actually ride this thing?' she asked, gripping
the broom with both hands. 'I mean, your
potion making's kind of questionable.'

Verity rolled her eyes. 'Can I ride this
thing?! Hold tight!'

There was a hushed, whooshing whisper. Grace just had time to tighten her grip before the ground disappeared beneath them.

She needn't have worried: Verity turned out to be a surprisingly good driver. Grace loosened her grip on the broom and began to enjoy the view.

Wondermere stretched out beneath her like a beautiful patchwork blanket. Fields rippled in waves of green felt, their furthest edges knitting up to scratchy grey strips of mountain. Velvet valleys dipped and rolled in every direction, stitched together by the darting blue thread of the River Mere.

'This is amazing!' Grace cried. 'I can't believe Dennis would rather swim than fly, he doesn't know what he's missing!'

'Looks like your unicorn's enjoying it, too,'
Verity said.

Grace watched as Poop overtook a fairy
plane, weaving in front of it, blasting flame
and sticking out his tongue at the passengers.

'So what's the plan?' Grace said, trying not
to look down. The market square was so far
away it looked no bigger than an envelope.

'I'll fly alongside him, as close as I can get,
then you jump across on to his back. He
should drop pretty quickly then.'

'*Drop?!*' Grace said, alarmed.

Verity ignored her. 'Nearly there,' she said,
closing in on Poop.

He gave Grace a pitiful look as a fresh
flurry of flame flickered from his rear end.

'We'll soon have you back on the ground,
boy,' she said, wishing she could reach him to

give him a reassuring pat. They were flying close beside him, but not close enough.

It was almost impossible to get the broomstick in the right position. Poop's bottom kept misfiring, making his flightpath impossible to predict. One minute he was trotting along in a fairly straight line, the next he'd shoot upwards, plummet several feet or else surprise them both by turning a loop the loop.

'Told you I was good at flying potions,' Verity said. 'This one's lasting ages!'

'We haven't *got* ages,' Grace complained.

'Don't get your Under-Wonders in a twist,' Verity said. 'I reckon I can get you close enough to jump across, and if you miss, I can probably catch you before you hit the ground ...'

'*Probably?!*' Grace said.

'It'll be a doddle for a champion troll-o player like you,' Verity said, manoeuvring the broom a little closer. 'Ready? On the count of three: One, two …'

'THREE!' Grace finished, leaping from the broom, arms pinwheeling as she reached for Poop's bridle.

'**GOAL!**' she yelled, landing squarely in his saddle.

'It's working!' Grace called up to Verity as Poop began to descend towards the ground. 'I can't believe it!'

'And I can't believe you ever doubted me,' Verity called back, following behind like a flapping black shadow. 'Look, there's your sister. I guess she sorted the potion already.'

Grace felt much safer in her familiar saddle than she had on the broomstick. She leaned over and peered at the ground. Tracks and trollways weaved through the trees like a crazy doodle. She soon spotted her sister, thundering along on Sprinkles in the direction of the tree house.

'Awesome,' Grace said, pointing Poop towards the distant turrets of Wondermere

Castle. 'She'll grab Dennis and be back at the castle in no time. Now let's make sure we're there to greet her!'

16

DO NOT GO SWIMMING IN ARMOUR

Poop may have loved being naughty, but he loved Grace too. He calmed down completely with his best friend at the reins.

They cruised at a steady height just above Wondermere Forest, occasionally catching a glimpse of Portia riding Sprinkles steadily through the trees. Bram sat behind her, one arm around her waist, the other cradling a small purple dragon.

'Up here!' Grace cried joyfully, waving back as she overtook them. **'IT'S AMAAZIING!'** The wind caught her words, whipping them away like whirling leaves.

She could see for miles, far further than she'd ever travelled, to where the land ended and the whole of Wondermere was bordered in blue. The Outer Ocean glowed orange as the sun began to set, giving her an unwelcome reminder of Queen Jeen. Would they really be able to get Dennis into his nest before the waterfolly started?

Verity drew her broomstick closer alongside her, casually filing her fingernails into points. 'Your unicorn's smoking.'

'Thanks,' said Grace proudly.

'No, I mean he's actually *smoking* – from

his bum. I think the potion's wearing off.'

Grace looked over her shoulder. Sure enough, green smoke was *putt-putt-putt*ing out from beneath Poop's tail. He let out a nervous whinny. 'Uh-oh,' Grace muttered as he began to drop at a rather alarming rate, hooves paddling the air limply.

Branches began to snag at Grace's boots. They'd never make it as far as the castle. They might not even make it past the last of the trees … She braced herself for a crash.

'Give up, boy,' Grace said. 'Whatever you do, *don't* make it past the trees!'

She hoped it would work. But would Poop still have the energy to disobey her? Yes! His ears pricked up and his legs began to pound the air once more. Grace felt a surge of relief. They were going to make it to the soft, grassy moat-side!

Poop snorted smugly as they cleared the final tree, but the ground was approaching at a crazy speed — and the moat-side was unexpectedly busy.

Tens of knights were standing around the water's edge, taking prime viewing positions before the waterfolly began. King Wonder and Taffy had taken up their spots on the drawbridge.

SPLOOSH!

CLONK!

CLASH!

At least the merfolk aren't in the water yet … Grace thought. With a bit of luck, there was still time to get Dennis safely into his nest before Queen Jeen set eyes on him.

But first there was the small matter of getting Poop safely *down*.

He landed gently enough – but he put the brakes on so quickly Grace went flying out of the saddle. 'Look out!' she yelled. Too late. She bumped into the nearest knight, knocking him over and sending the others toppling like dominoes.

CLANG!

BANG!

King Wonder lost his balance and toppled head first into the moat. 'Oops,' Grace said, getting shakily to her feet. Verity landed her broomstick softly beside her, but no one noticed. They were all too busy looking at the king.

'What leadership, your majesty!' said Taffy Trafalgar, bouncing around in glee. 'We should *all* show the merfolk our willingness to participate in waterfolly!' The old troll dived into the moat, followed by the tumbled knights, who struggled to remove their armour before leaping in.

'Psst!' Grace spun around. Portia had arrived on Sprinkles. She was hiding behind the nearest tree with Bram, who was keeping a tight hold of Dennis. As soon as the little dragon spotted Grace he tried to reach her, wriggling against Bram's grip. **'MEEP!'**

'Aww,' said Verity, 'is this your dragon? What a cutie!'

'He may be cute, but he's also strong,' Bram said. 'He's been flapping and fidgeting the whole way!'

'Let me hold him,' said Portia. She took hold of Dennis, flinching as his flailing wing knocked her glasses off her face.

'We'll never get the potion in him if he keeps wriggling. Maybe he'll calm down if Grace holds him,' said Bram, turning his attention to the exhausted unicorns.

'Come to Mummy, Dennis,' Grace said, letting him clamber into her arms. He did settle down, although every now and then his little body twitched and tugged in the direction of the moat. 'I swear he'd head right for the water if I let go of him.'

'Seems like a popular choice,' Portia said, watching as the moat churned with thrashing, splashing knights. 'What's going on with that lot?'

Grace was about to explain the impact of her landing when Sir Arthur came hopping along the moat-side, still trying to remove his boots. 'Just in time, princesses,' he said cheerfully. 'The waterfolly showcase is about to begin!'

Sir Oliver came over to greet the princesses too, wrestling his way out of his chainmail. 'The merfolk are on their way from the royal baths,' he said excitedly. 'It seems your father wants us not just to spectate, but to join in. As you wish, great leader – **CANNONBAAAAALL!**'

The boys plunged into the moat.

Portia watched in disbelief. 'Did Dad *really* order them all to jump in?'

'It's my fault.' Grace grimaced. 'I may have accidentally dunked him.'

King Wonder dragged himself to the edge of the moat, coughing and spluttering. 'If I find out I'm wet because of you …' he began wearily.

Grace looked around desperately for a place to hide Dennis, but it was too late. The king had spotted him. His expression grew even darker. 'What did I tell you about that *thing*?'

Grace pretended not to hear. 'Hey, it looks like you've inspired the whole troll-o team to get excited about waterfolly,' she said. 'Well done!'

The king glared at her. 'Flattery won't help, young lady. You're in very big trouble this time.'

Grace didn't have time to worry about what her punishment might be. She was more concerned with keeping hold of Dennis, who was struggling harder than ever to break free. 'He's trying to get to the moat again ...'

'He's trying to get himself locked in the dungeon!' King Wonder growled. 'Why is Dennis still here? Get rid of him, now! The merfolk will be out here any minute. If Queen Jeen sees him ...'

'She won't,' Grace said firmly. 'He'll be safely up in his nest, just like all the other dragons. Out of the way and absolutely not a problem. Trust us, Dad. We've been busy working it all out and it'll be sorted in a second, honest.'

'You promise?'

Grace put a hand to her chest. 'Knight's honour.' It was the strongest promise she could possibly make. She only hoped she could keep it.

17

DO NOT
GIVE UP

Dennis was still trying to claw his way
towards the moat.

'If he ends up in the water, Queen Jeen will
flip,' Grace said, struggling to keep hold of
him. 'We have to get that potion in him, fast.'

'Here it is,' Portia said, taking a bottle
out of her dress pocket. 'I followed the
instructions to the letter.'

'Looks OK, I guess,' Verity said sniffily, 'but I would have done it better.'

Bram laughed. 'No you wouldn't! Your potions always go wrong. Anyway, does your gran know you've been flying your broomstick? I thought you were supposed to be grounded?'

'Shh!' Verity hissed, looking around shiftily.

'Grounded?' Portia said anxiously. 'We wouldn't want to get you in any trouble ...'

'It's no biggie, Gran just gets a bit uptight about some of my magic.'

'I'm not surprised,' Bram said. 'You gave her antlers!'

Grace's eyes grew round. 'Is that why she wasn't running the stall today?'

Verity shrugged. 'So? They suit her, plus

she's always complaining she has nowhere to hang her cloak. Anyway, I'm a perfectly capable witch, as was evident from my amazing flying potion.'

'*My* amazing flying potion,' Grace said.

'Farting potion, more like,' Verity said under her breath.

'Stop squabbling,' Portia said, pulling out the stopper. 'This batch is *my* amazing flying potion, following the exact recipe in the book. Now let's hope it works …'

'It had better work,' said King Wonder crossly.

'Of course it'll work,' Grace said confidently, taking the bottle. 'Go get ready to watch the waterfolly, Dad. We'll join you on the drawbridge as soon as Dennis is safely in his nest.'

'Don't mess this up,' he said, before storming away.

'No pressure,' Verity said, rolling her eyes.

Grace took a deep breath, waited for Dennis's next *meep*, then tipped the whole lot into his open beak. 'Drink up, little fella, it's time you learned to use those wings.'

The effect was immediate. Dennis stopped struggling and fell limp in Grace's arms. 'Is he all right?' Bram asked, giving the little dragon a worried look.

'Maybe you didn't mix it right?' Verity said.

'Oh, no,' Portia said. 'What if I've hurt him?'

But Dennis's wings gave a little flutter. Grace grinned as his scaly body wriggled and began to lift, slowly but surely, out of her arms. 'He's doing it! He's flying!'

Dennis gave Grace an astonished look as his wings began to flap, seemingly of their own accord, beating out a steady rhythm in the air. **'MEEP?!'** he squeaked, hovering above his friends and testing out his new skills. **'MEEP-MEEP!'**

Just then, a trumpet blared from the castle gates, startling the little dragon right out of the air. Grace caught him, holding him tightly as the merfolk's chariots wheeled out of the castle and on to the drawbridge.

'Ooh,' Verity said, 'is that Queen Jeen? How can you not like her? She looks super cool to me.'

Grace could see Verity's point. Wielding her waterfolly stick and proudly leading her squad to the water, the merqueen *did* look pretty awesome. Brooke, Marlin and their squadmates watched their leader intently as she selected the best spot to enter the moat. On her cue they all dived in eagerly, Queen Jeen slipping in after them with a flick of her tail. She must be feeling the same way Grace did when she led her troll-o team on to the pitch …

'Quick,' Portia said, 'we have to get Dennis into his nest before she sees him!'

'I could try the catapult thing again?' Bram said, panicking and turning himself into a watering can.

'There's no time,' Grace said. 'Come on, Dennis, let's do this.' She grabbed Verity's broom, swung a leg over it and kicked off the ground.

18

DO NOT FORGET YOUR TISSUES

Grace went the long way round, flying around the back of the castle. She was out of sight from the merfolk and the ever-growing crowd of spectators. She was out of sight from her father on the drawbridge, too.

But it wasn't just King Wonder and Queen Jeen she was hiding from. She didn't want to say goodbye to Dennis in front of Portia and her friends.

She knew she'd see him again, every day probably, but only ever from a distance. She smiled sadly, feeling the warmth of his little body against hers for what would surely be the very last time.

Once she reached the back of the castle, Grace flew up over the walls, getting a good view of some of Dennis's neighbours in their nests. He began to purr as he caught sight of them. His tail wagged, causing the broom to wobble.

'Steady on, Dennis!' Grace cried, her heart hammering as they took a dive towards the cobbled courtyard below. She regained control, pulling the broom up again and pointing it at Dennis's nest.

'Do you remember being an egg?' she wondered out loud. 'More importantly, will your parents remember *you*?'

They were about to find out. Grace slowed down as she approached the turret, then brought the broomstick to a hover beside the nest. She was careful to stay inside the castle walls, out of sight. But she wasn't out of sight of the dragons.

'Special delivery,' she called out softly. She held her breath as not one but two enormous heads reared up out of the nest, staring at her through narrowed eyes.

'MEEP!' Dennis couldn't flap his wings fast enough. He tugged himself free from Grace's grip and flung himself away, flapping unsteadily towards his gigantic parents. The larger of the two took one look at Dennis

and sneezed dismissively, blowing him off course.

Undeterred, Dennis flapped harder, flying back towards his parents in his own wonky, winding way.

For one terrible moment Grace thought the adult dragons were going to swat him out of the sky. She needn't have worried. The smaller dragon reared up, opened its wings

out wide and began to purr. The other dragon softened its stance and joined in, welcoming Dennis with a tender bump of its giant beak. Their purrs were so loud Grace thought the resulting rumbling might shake the turret to pieces.

She watched, delighted, as Dennis's parents fussed over their son. The plan had worked! Dennis was where he belonged. He seemed well and truly at home, finally looking comfortable in his own scaly skin. Grace knew she ought to be happy for him, and she was. But at the same time it felt like an ogre had wrapped its hands around her heart and wouldn't stop squeezing.

'Bye, Dennis,' she said quietly. 'I'll miss you.'

Dennis didn't even hear. He was too busy tumbling happily around his nest. Grace wiped a tear on her sleeve and flew silently back to her friends.

19

DO NOT THROW
THE BALL BACK

The crowd was still growing. It seemed the
whole realm was keen to witness the
exhibition match.

Most Wondermerians had heard of
waterfolly, but few had ever watched it. So
far as Grace understood, it was a sort of
acrobatic, water-based version of troll-o, only
using nets instead of mallets and giant

pearls instead of ball-trolls. Grace couldn't
see the appeal, but clearly everyone else felt
differently.

They flocked from forest and fields,
trudging down tracks and crammed into
carts, forming a disorderly ring around the
castle moat.

Even the shy giants had turned up, sitting
side by side with hobgoblins on picnic
blankets, forcing wizards and farmers to
stand on their carts for a better view over
their towering heads. Whole fairy families
flitted to the front, fitting easily between
their larger neighbours.

A band of boggarts struck up a rousing
rendition of an old Wondermerian troll-o
chant, and Grace found herself humming
along. The thought of troll-o cheered her

up a little as she steered the broomstick back to its owner.

'Thanks for the lend,' she said, handing it back to Verity. She thought Verity might be cross that she'd taken it without asking, but it seemed the witch was enjoying the festivities too much to care.

'I'd have missed this if it wasn't for you two,' she said. 'Gran would ground me until next Christmas if she knew I was here!'

'VERITY MERRIWINKLE!' The voice came from behind them, sudden and sharp, making Grace jump. She spun around, coming face to face with an old, antlered woman.

'Hi, Gran,' said Verity weakly, handing over her broomstick without even being asked. 'I know, I'm grounded.'

Her grandmother took the broomstick and began using it to shoo her granddaughter back towards the forest. 'You're double grounded now,' she said. 'No flying until next Christmas!'

'Wait,' Portia called after them, 'it's not Verity's fault!'

'It's true, Mother Merriwinkle,' Bram agreed. 'She was helping the princesses with, erm …

important royal business.'

The old lady stopped in her tracks. 'Verity?' she said incredulously. '*Helping?*'

'Knight's honour,' Grace said. 'In fact, Verity's been *such* a help she's welcome to join us on the drawbridge as our special guest for tonight's exhibition match. That is, if it's all right with you?'

'Absolutely.' The old witch bowed her head, forcing Grace to jump out of the way of her antlers. 'Back before midnight, Verity, or I'll turn your bed into a pumpkin!'

King Wonder was absolutely delighted to see his daughters, in spite of the lack of frilly dresses and the additions of dirt, a stable boy and a trainee witch. The reason for his good cheer? 'No dragon!'

'That's right,' Grace said, trying to sound happy about it, 'Dennis is back in his nest, as promised.'

Her father wrapped his arms around her and lifted her briefly off the ground. 'Well done, Grace. I know that won't have been easy for you. But look! It was definitely worth it. Now you get to be here to enjoy the waterfolly!'

'Great,' said Grace, rather unconvincingly.

But the more she watched, the more

enthralled she
became.

The merfolk
were totally
astounding in
the water. They
darted about like
arrows, chasing
after the huge pearl as it
was tossed skilfully from
net to net between members
of the opposing squad. The
pearl was only ever passed
to another player above water,
giving the other squad a chance to
intercept. Once a player had
caught the pearl, they would dive
beneath the surface, tail speeding

them around the moat to complete a lap and score a point.

Fins flipped, nets flung, sticks struck and the water frothed furiously as the whole squad raced, chased and battled for victory. Queen Jeen herself was an excellent player, helping her side score point after point.

At half-time, Grace took a deep breath, swallowed her pride and leaned over the drawbridge. 'OK, so that was actually really cool,' she said honestly.

Queen Jeen arched an eyebrow. 'As cool as troll-o?'

'Almost.' Grace grinned. 'You know, you have a very impressive swing. You should give troll-o a go, I reckon you'd be pretty handy with a mallet.'

Now it was Queen Jeen's turn to smile.

With Dennis out of the picture, the merqueen was relaxed, chatty and surprisingly good company. Grace had a thoroughly enjoyable time discussing tactics with her until the second half began. Maybe this visit wouldn't be so awful after all.

'See, princess?' said Taffy Trafalgar happily as they settled down to watch the second half. 'It's really very much like troll-o!'

'Grace and Queen Jeen have a lot in common,' the king agreed. 'This really is the most remarkable opportunity to …'

But Grace wasn't listening. She was watching the match intently, never once taking her eyes off the pearl – and right now it was flying towards her father's face like a cannonball.

'Look out!' Portia squealed, but Grace was swift. She stuck out an arm, grabbing the pearl in mid-air. The king gulped. Taffy swooned. The entire crowd cheered. Even Queen Jeen led her squad in giving Grace a huge round of applause.

'It seems the skills of a troll-o knight are worthy after all,' the merqueen said teasingly. 'I look forward to seeing your own exhibition match at the soonest opportunity.'

'Tomorrow?' Grace said hopefully.

'Tomorrow,' her new friend agreed. 'Now can we please have our ball back?'

'Sure thing,' Grace said with a grin. She drew her arm back and let the pearl fly, yelling, **'FETCH!'**

It only took the briefest of moments for her to realise her mistake.

The crowd pointed and gasped as a tiny dragon shot out of its nest, turning a triple somersault and giving a triumphant,

'MEEP!'

'Get back in your nest,' Grace breathed, *'please!'* It was no use. Dennis was clearly delighted with his newfound powers — and even more delighted to have such a large audience.

'MEEP-MEEP!'

he cried, paused in mid-air

for one dreadful, heart-stopping moment,

then torpedoed into the water with an

almighty **SPLOOSH!**

20

DO NOT BE AFRAID TO ADMIT YOU WERE WRONG

Dennis erupted triumphantly out of the water, hovering above the surface and carrying the pearl in his beak.

'It's back!' Queen Jeen shrieked. 'That hideous creature is back – and it's turned the water purple!'

Grace's shoulders slumped. 'Here we go again!'

'EXPLAIN YOURSELF, GRACE WONDER!' the king roared.

Grace felt defeated. The royal visit was
well and truly ruined. But right now, she was
more concerned about Dennis. He looked
utterly bewildered, clearly confused about
why no one was praising him for his brilliant
fetch.

The poor little dragon flapped his wings and looked down, astonished, at the merfolk splashing about in panic beneath him. 'Bring the pearl here, Dennis,' Grace said. 'Who's a good dragon?'

He flew obediently to the drawbridge, dropped the pearl into her hands and wagged his tail, eager to perform his trick again.

'What in all Wonder ... ?' the king began.

'You *trained* him?' the merqueen spluttered.

'He isn't a *hideous creature*,' Grace said firmly. 'He's brilliant, and he really loves water, just like you. Watch this – Dennis, fetch!'

Grace dropped the pearl over the edge of the drawbridge. Dennis dived after it, sending the merfolk reeling, but he bobbed back up with the pearl, looking delighted with himself. 'Now take it to the nice lady, Dennis.'

Dennis gave Grace a doubtful look, then plunged beneath the surface, tail wagging, powering him across the moat to Queen Jeen.

Grace watched his sleek form slipping effortlessly along beneath the water. He weaved his way between the cowering merfolk to their leader, circling her rapidly before – **SPLASH!** He bobbed up like a cork, depositing the pearl in the merqueen's trembling hands. **'MEEP!'**

Dennis hovered above the moat, bottom wiggling. 'What's it doing?!' Queen Jeen said.

Grace shrugged. 'He wants you to throw it.' **'MEEP!'**

'He ... he won't hurt me?'

Taffy Trafalgar cleared his throat and

raised his ears high. 'There are no recorded instances of dragons harming anyone in all Wondermerian history.'

'None recorded *yet*,' Queen Jeen said, screwing her face up as Dennis gave it a big friendly lick.

Portia laughed. 'Dennis won't hurt you – he's a sweetheart!'

'He just wants to play,' Grace added. 'I think he's been enjoying watching the waterfolly as much as we have.'

Queen Jeen's face broke into a radiant smile. King Wonder was busy opening and closing his mouth like a landed fish. He looked even more astonished as the merqueen popped the pearl into her net, swung it artfully back and let it fly.

'FETCH!' she yelled. Dennis flung himself

after the pearl, diving gracefully under the water to retrieve it. The merqueen let out a whoop of delight, punching the air in triumph. 'Well done, that dragon!'

'I told you!' Grace said. 'Dennis is a legend!'

Seeing their queen embrace the new addition to the game, the other merfolk dived after Dennis, swimming alongside and around him, trying to retrieve the pearl with their nets. Brooke managed to snatch it away before swiftly passing it to Marlin. Dennis immediately gave chase, forked tongue poking out in concentration as he focused his attention on the pearl. It was unclear which side Dennis thought he was on, but he certainly kept the merfolk on their fins. The squad were having the time of their lives.

Soon the whole crowd was cheering wildly as the game became even more unpredictable – and even more entertaining. 'Waterfolly fever has well and truly arrived in Wondermere,' Taffy said, hopping happily around.

'Well done, girls,' King Wonder said warmly, wrapping his arms around his daughters. 'I should never have doubted my two best knights.'

Grace grinned at her sister.

'BEST ROYAL VISIT EVER.'

21

WONDERS
NEVER CEASE!

As promised, the troll-o exhibition match took place the very next day – but only after Grace and Portia had introduced the merfolk to the benefits of a lie-in. They also found time to introduce their guests to the joy of bashed waffles, followed by a spot of dragon-watching and a tour of the royal stables.

The whole day went brilliantly,

particularly the troll-o, which drew just as large a crowd as the waterfolly. The girls were delighted to see Verity waving at them happily from the grandstands along with her grandmother. Grace couldn't help but wonder if the older witch knew there was a sparkling **'GO TEAM RED'** banner slung between her antlers.

The merfolk held up banners too, watching from their water-filled chariots at the edge of the pitch. They cheered with delight as they followed every pass, dodge and whack of the ball-troll.

Queen Jeen enjoyed the match thoroughly, the only slight dampener being when, confusing her hair for bogweed, Poop left the pitch, ambled over to her chariot and started trying to eat it.

'I'm willing to accept that these dragons of yours are rather special,' the merqueen said, shaking hands with the players once the match was over, 'but that unicorn of yours is something else.'

King Wonder winced, worried that Grace would take offence. But instead she shook their visitor's hand, bowed low and said, 'You're not wrong there.'

'Excuse me a moment,' said Queen Jeen, 'the Outer Ocean is calling.' She lifted a fist-sized shell out of her chariot and put it to her ear, listening intently.

'We're needed at home,' she said a little sadly. 'It's time we said our goodbyes.'

The Wonders accompanied their guests to the castle gates, where they spent a few happy minutes watching Dennis play in the moat. 'Look, your highness,' said Portia to Queen Jeen, laughing and pointing up to his nest, 'Dennis's parents look just like you did when you first met him!'

It was true. Dennis's parents looked utterly bemused and not a little bit appalled by his un-dragon-like behaviour. Dennis wasn't bothered in the slightest. He soared up out of the water to greet them both with a happy **'MEEP!'** before diving back in.

He was having so much fun he didn't even notice the merfolk leaving. The princesses said their goodbyes, waving until the chariots eventually slipped out of sight. Grace was surprised how sorry she felt to see the visitors go. But she soon cheered up as she turned her attention back to Dennis.

She watched contentedly as he scooted along on the moat's surface, wings paddling him along in a lazy backstroke. 'He's certainly one of a kind,' said King Wonder.

'Aren't we all?' Grace said.

'Congratulations, Sir Grace,' said Taffy. 'I'd say you made this royal visit the most memorable one on record.

Grace smiled, but she hadn't done it on purpose.

The truth was she'd just followed her heart, and right now her heart felt fit to burst. She was happy – beyond happy. Her sister and her friends were beside her, including her sore-bottomed unicorn and her slightly bonkers baby dragon. Who knew what other incredible, unusual and complicated people they might encounter next?

Grace grinned and took her sister's hand. The whole realm was theirs to discover, one epic quest at a time.

'MEEP! MEEP!'